W9-ATB-038

LIBRARY OF DOOM

GRAPHIC NOVELS

SPELL-BOUND

TEXT BY
STEVE BREZENOFF

ART BY
JUAN CALLE

COLORS BY
LUIS SUAREZ (LIBERUM DONUM)

STONE ARCH BOOKS
a capstone imprint

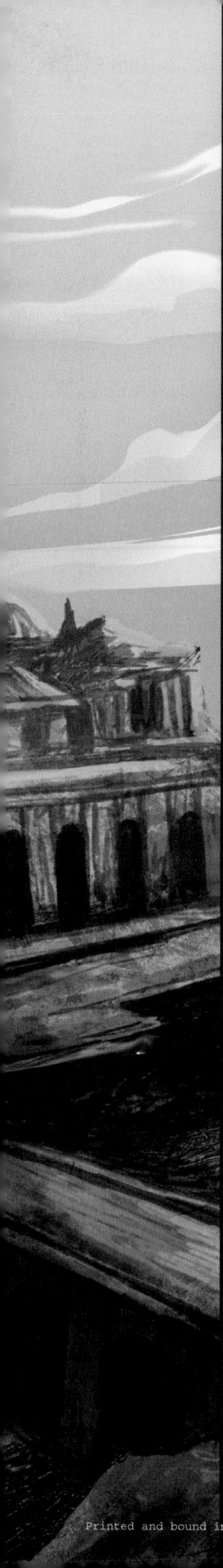

Published by Stone Arch Books, an imprint of Capstone
1710 Roe Crest Drive, North Mankato, Minnesota 56003
capstonepub.com

Library of Congress Cataloging-in-Publication Data is available on the Library of Congress website.

ISBN: 9781666346299 (hardcover)
ISBN: 9781666346312 (paperback)
ISBN: 9781666346329 (ebook PDF)

Summary: A student cramming for her spelling test picks up a vocabulary book cursed by the evil wizard Spellbinder. It'll be up to the mighty Librarian to help the girl escape the deadly tangle of terms before it's too late.

Designer: Hilary Wacholz
Editor: Abby Huff

This series of graphic novels is dedicated to
the memory of Brandon Terrell. I thought of him
often while writing these stories. –SB

Printed and bound in the USA. PO4882

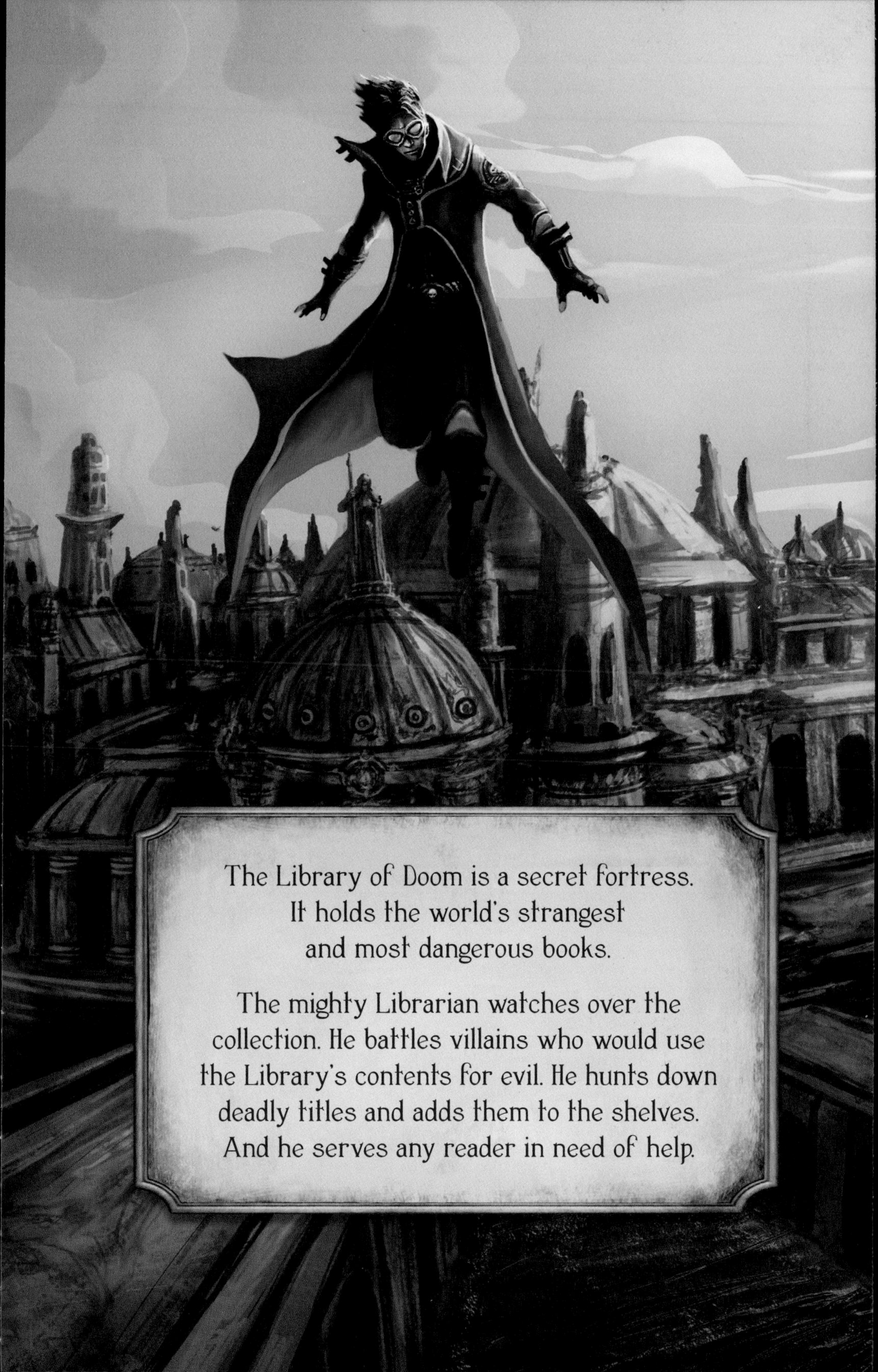

The Library of Doom is a secret fortress. It holds the world's strangest and most dangerous books.

The mighty Librarian watches over the collection. He battles villains who would use the Library's contents for evil. He hunts down deadly titles and adds them to the shelves. And he serves any reader in need of help.

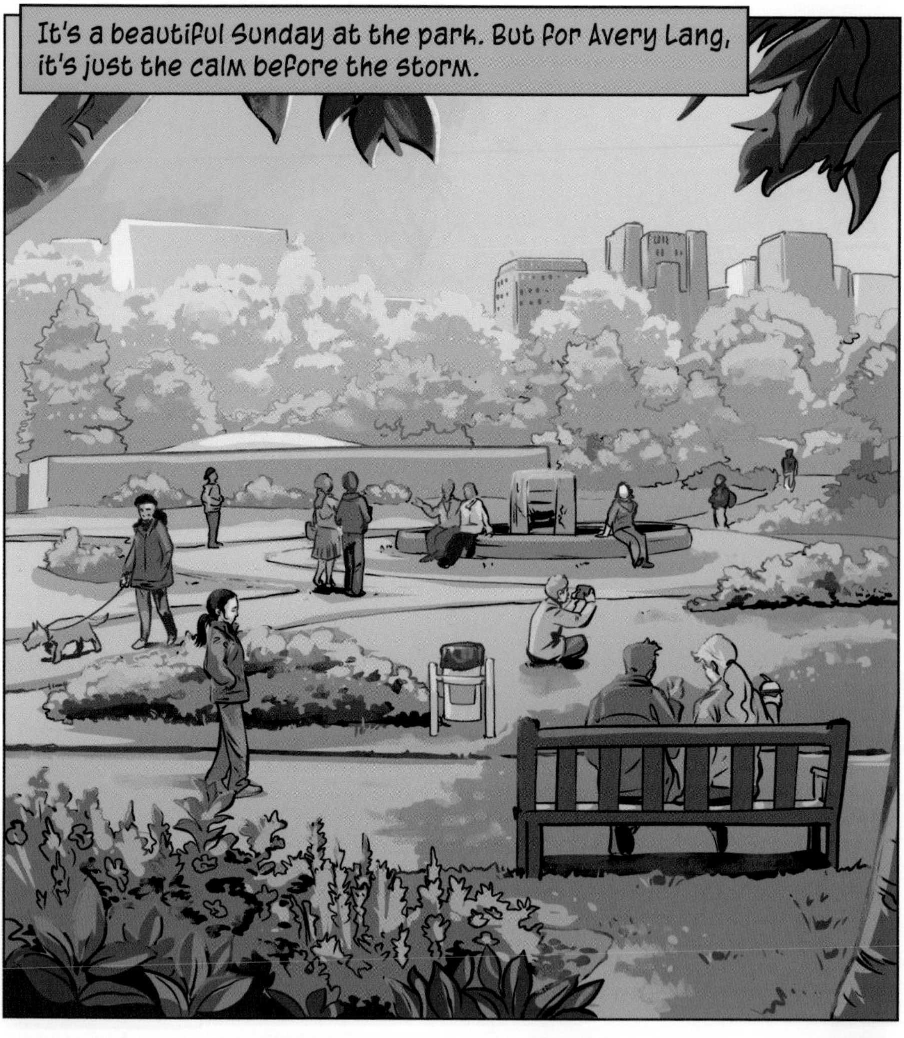
It's a beautiful Sunday at the park. But for Avery Lang, it's just the calm before the storm.

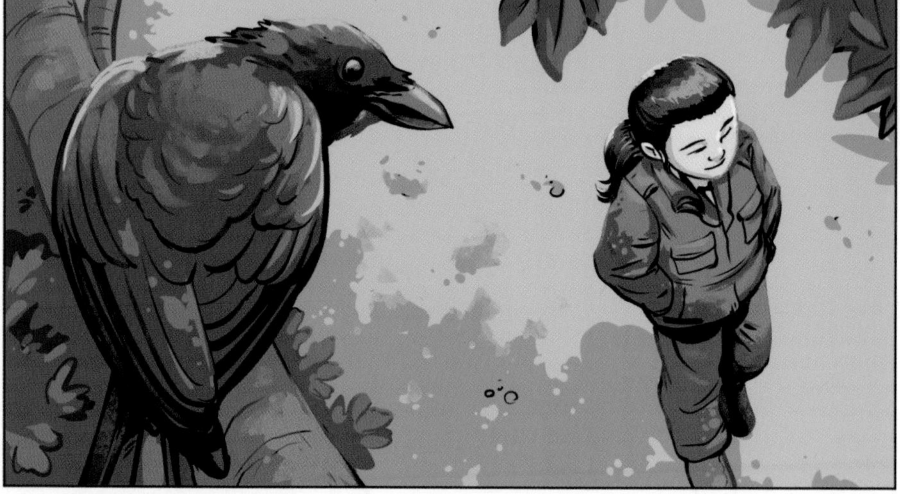

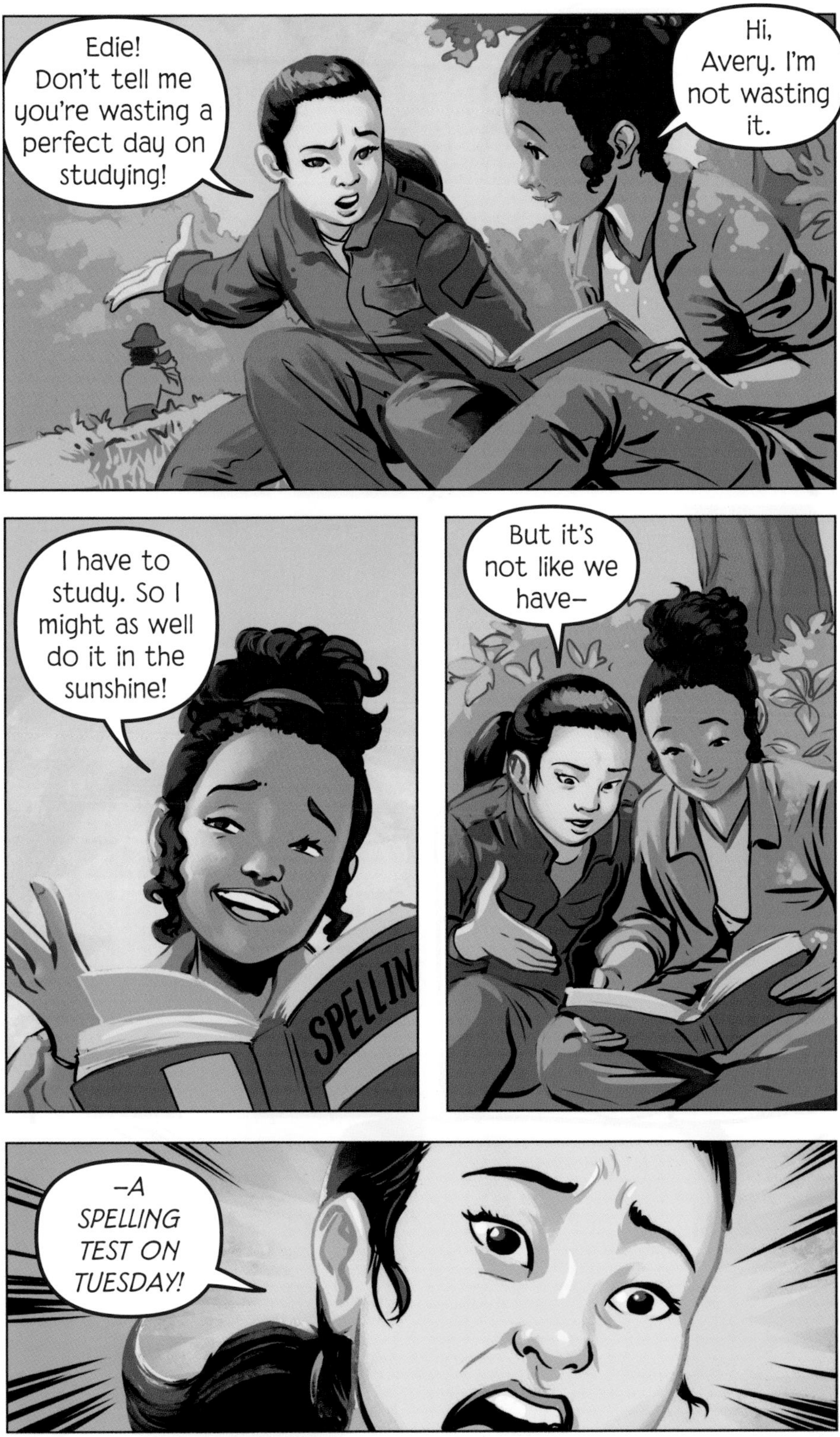
Edie! Don't tell me you're wasting a perfect day on studying!
Hi, Avery. I'm not wasting it.
I have to study. So I might as well do it in the sunshine!
SPELLIN
But it's not like we have–
–A SPELLING TEST ON TUESDAY!

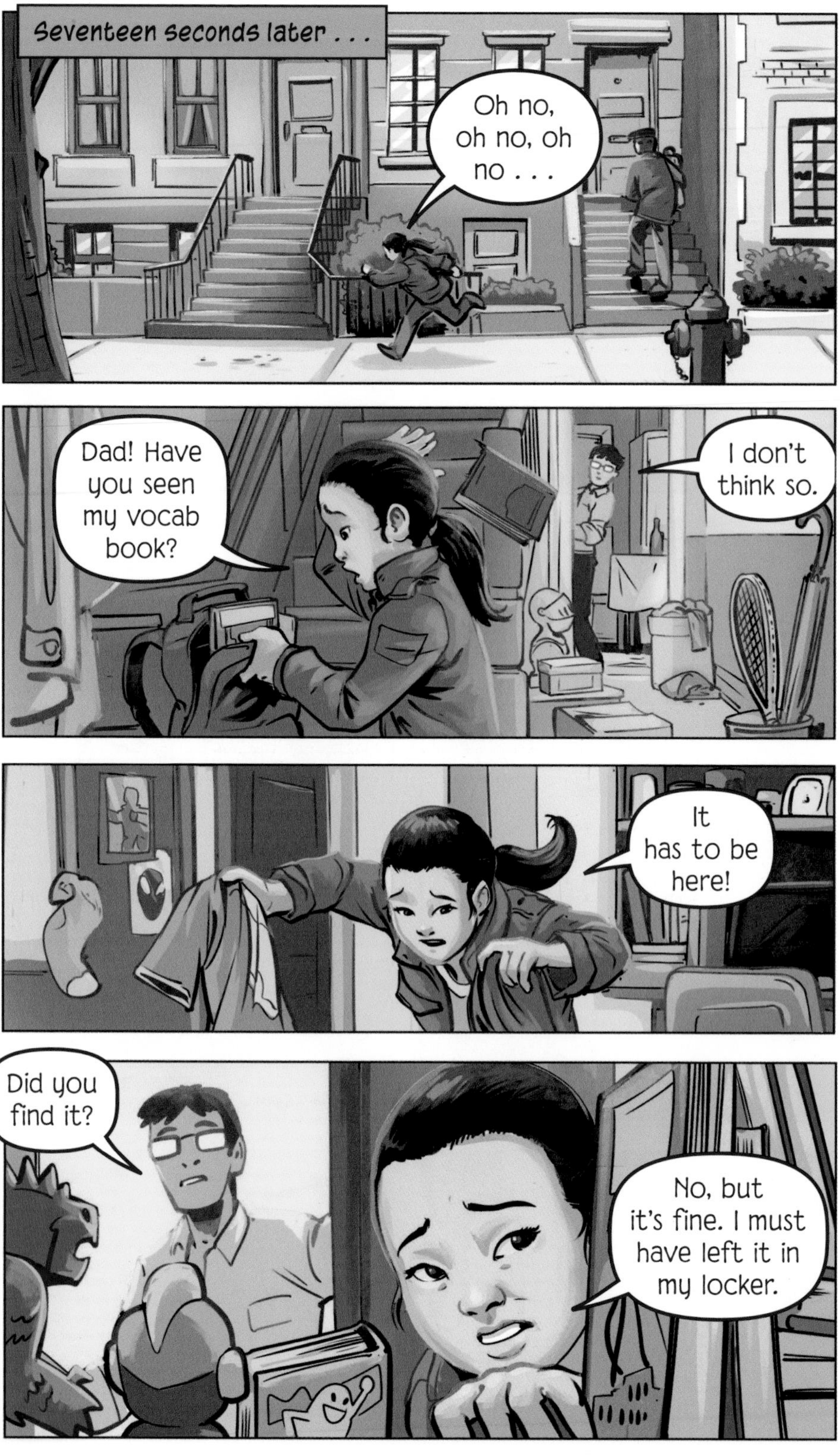
Seventeen seconds later . . .
Oh no, oh no, oh no . . .
Dad! Have you seen my vocab book?
I don't think so.
It has to be here!
Did you find it?
No, but it's fine. I must have left it in my locker.

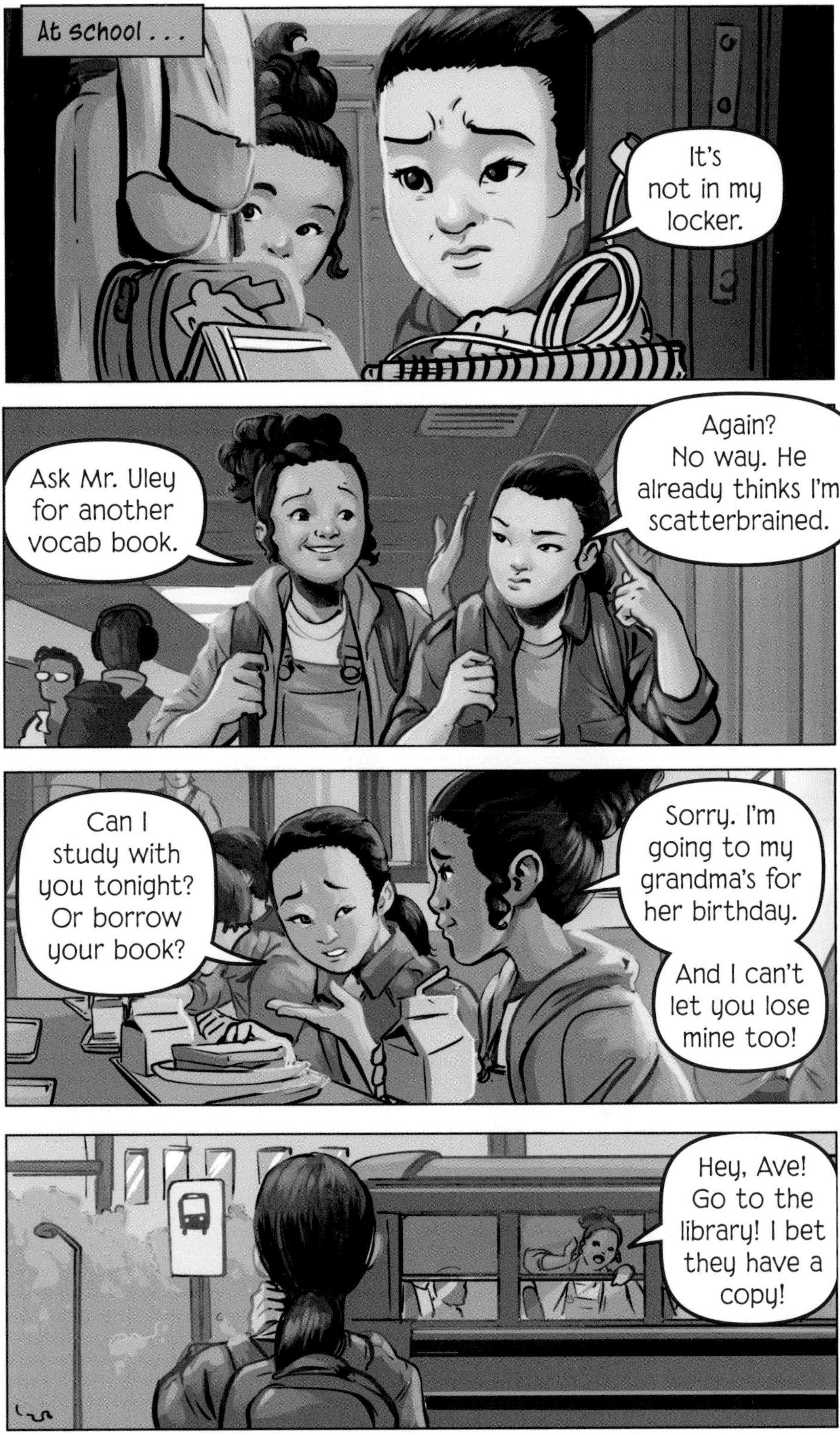
At school . . .
It's not in my locker.
Ask Mr. Uley for another vocab book.
Again? No way. He already thinks I'm scatterbrained.
Can I study with you tonight? Or borrow your book?
Sorry. I'm going to my grandma's for her birthday.
And I can't let you lose mine too!
Hey, Ave! Go to the library! I bet they have a copy!

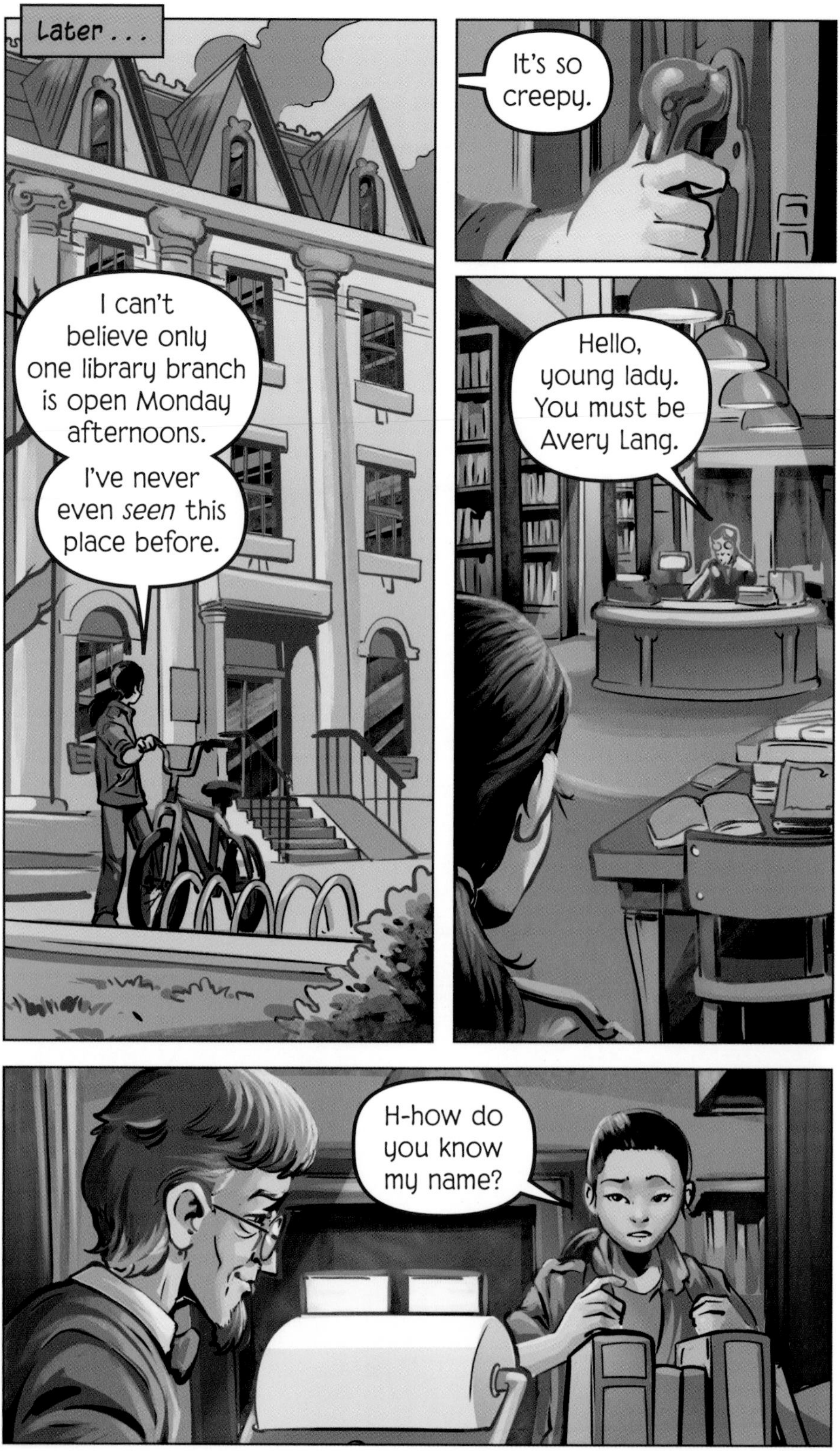
Later . . .
I can't believe only one library branch is open Monday afternoons.
I've never even *seen* this place before.
It's so creepy.
Hello, young lady. You must be Avery Lang.
H-how do you know my name?

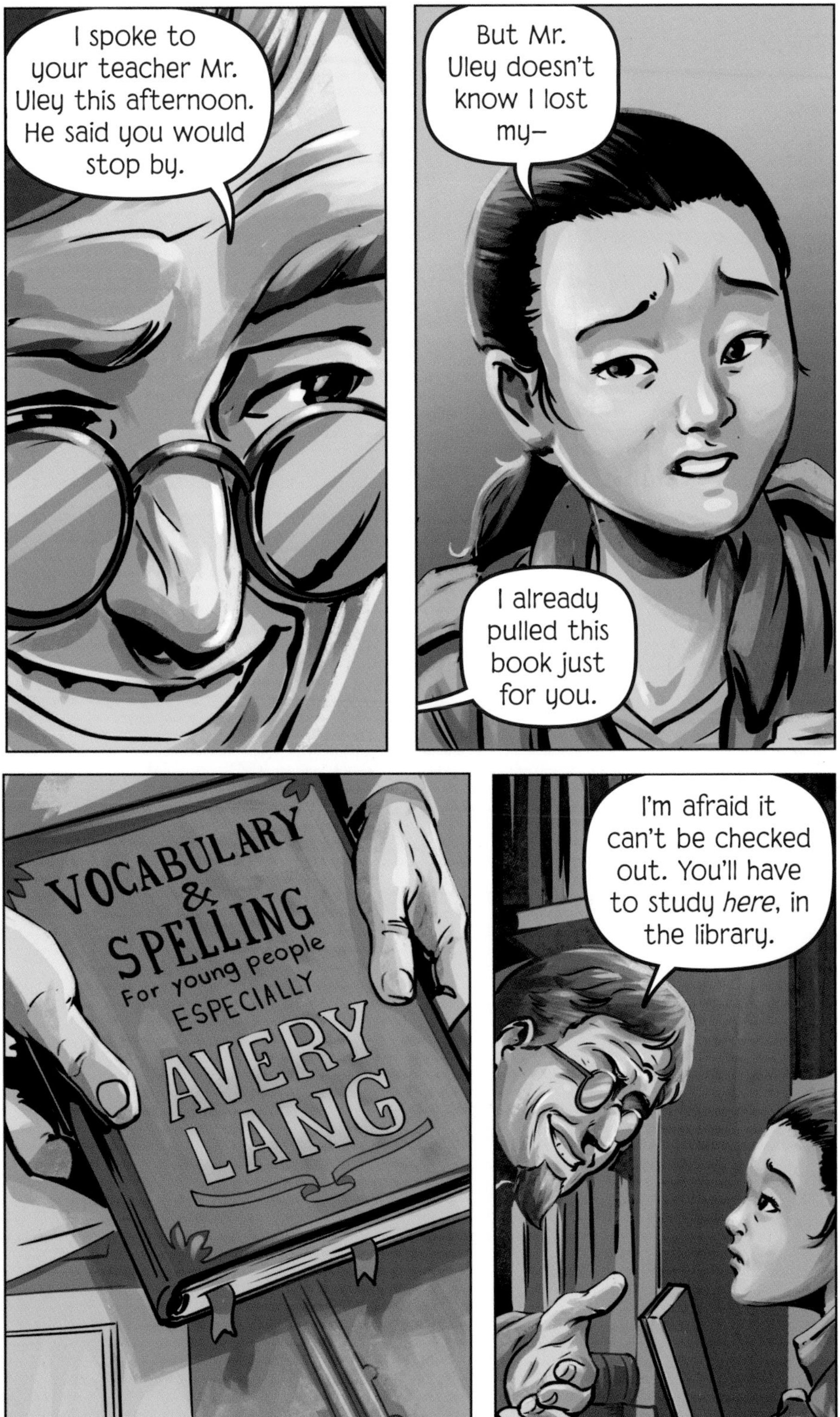
I spoke to your teacher Mr. Uley this afternoon. He said you would stop by.
But Mr. Uley doesn't know I lost my–
I already pulled this book just for you.
VOCABULARY & SPELLING For young people ESPECIALLY AVERY LANG
I'm afraid it can't be checked out. You'll have to study *here*, in the library.

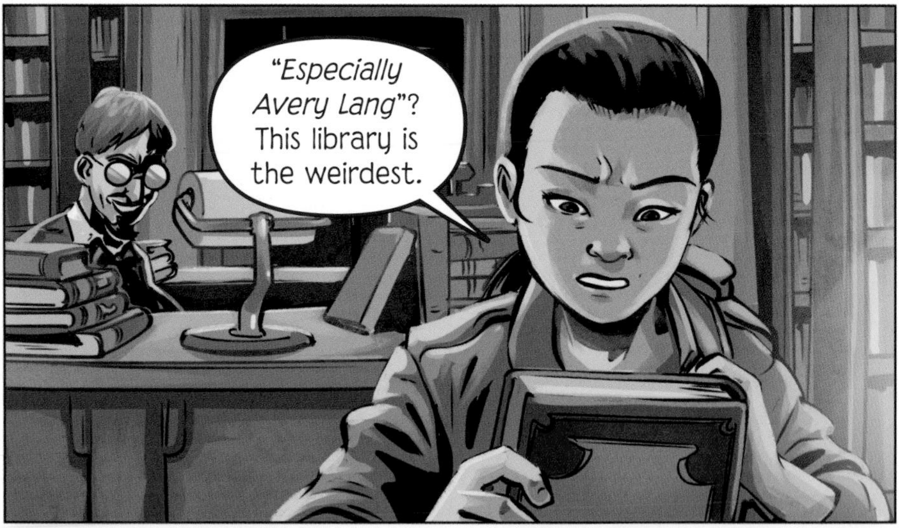
"*Especially Avery Lang*"? This library is the weirdest.

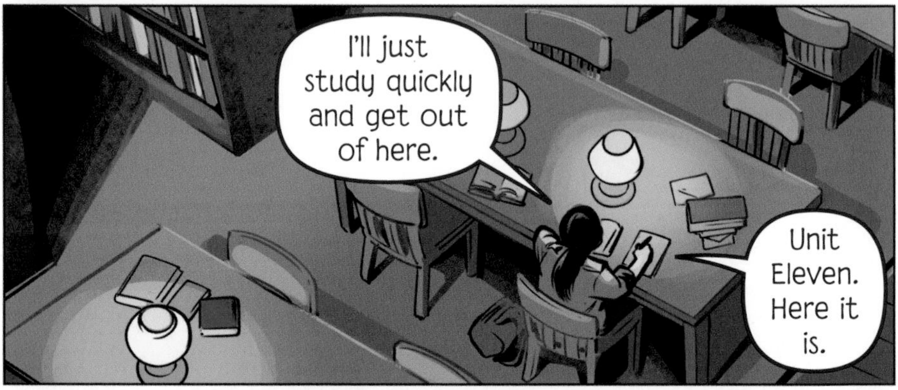
I'll just study quickly and get out of here.
Unit Eleven. Here it is.

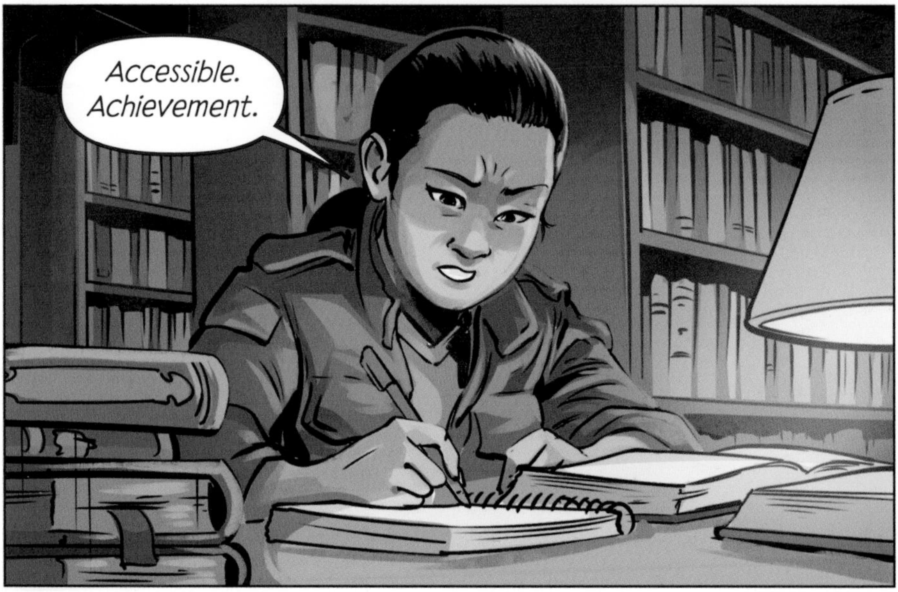
Accessible. Achievement.

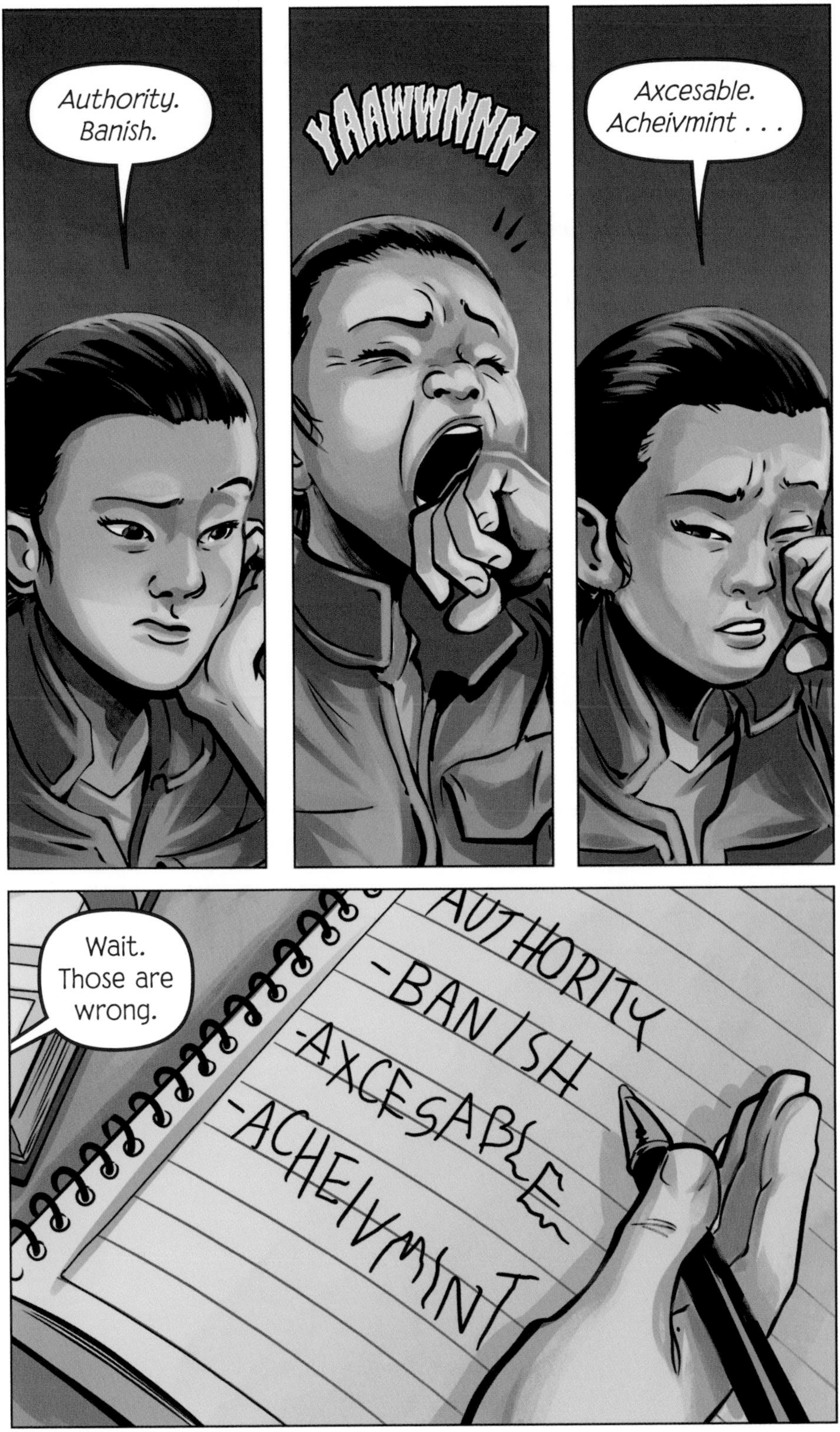
Authority.
Banish.
YAAWWNNN
Axcesable.
Acheivmint . . .
Wait. Those are wrong.
AUTHORITY
-BANISH
-AXCESABLE
-ACHEIVMINT

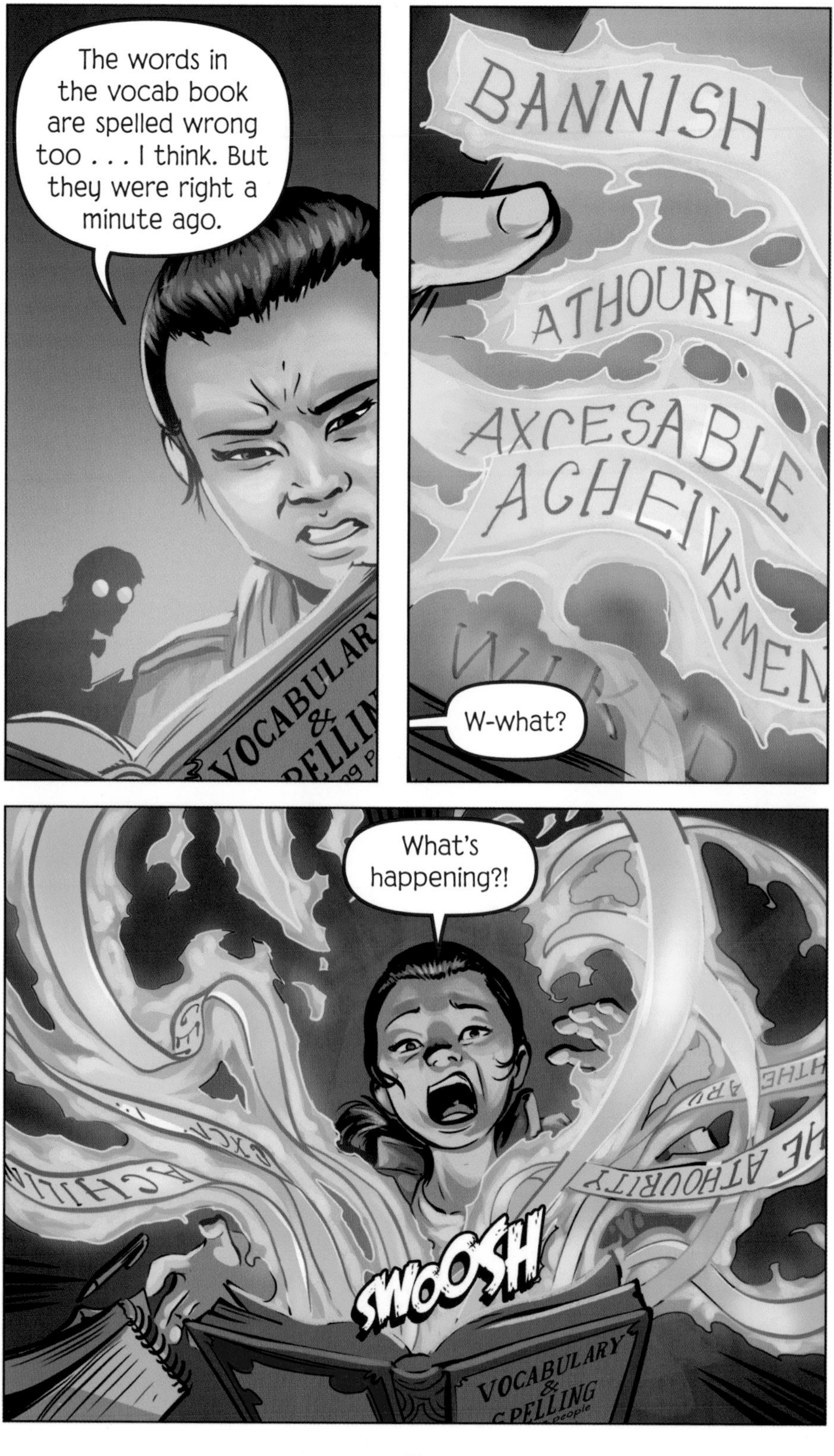
The words in the vocab book are spelled wrong too . . . I think. But they were right a minute ago.
VOCABULARY & SPELLING
BANNISH
ATHOURITY
AXCESABLE
ACHEIVEMEN
W-what?
What's happening?!
HE ATHOURITY
SWOOSH
VOCABULARY & SPELLING

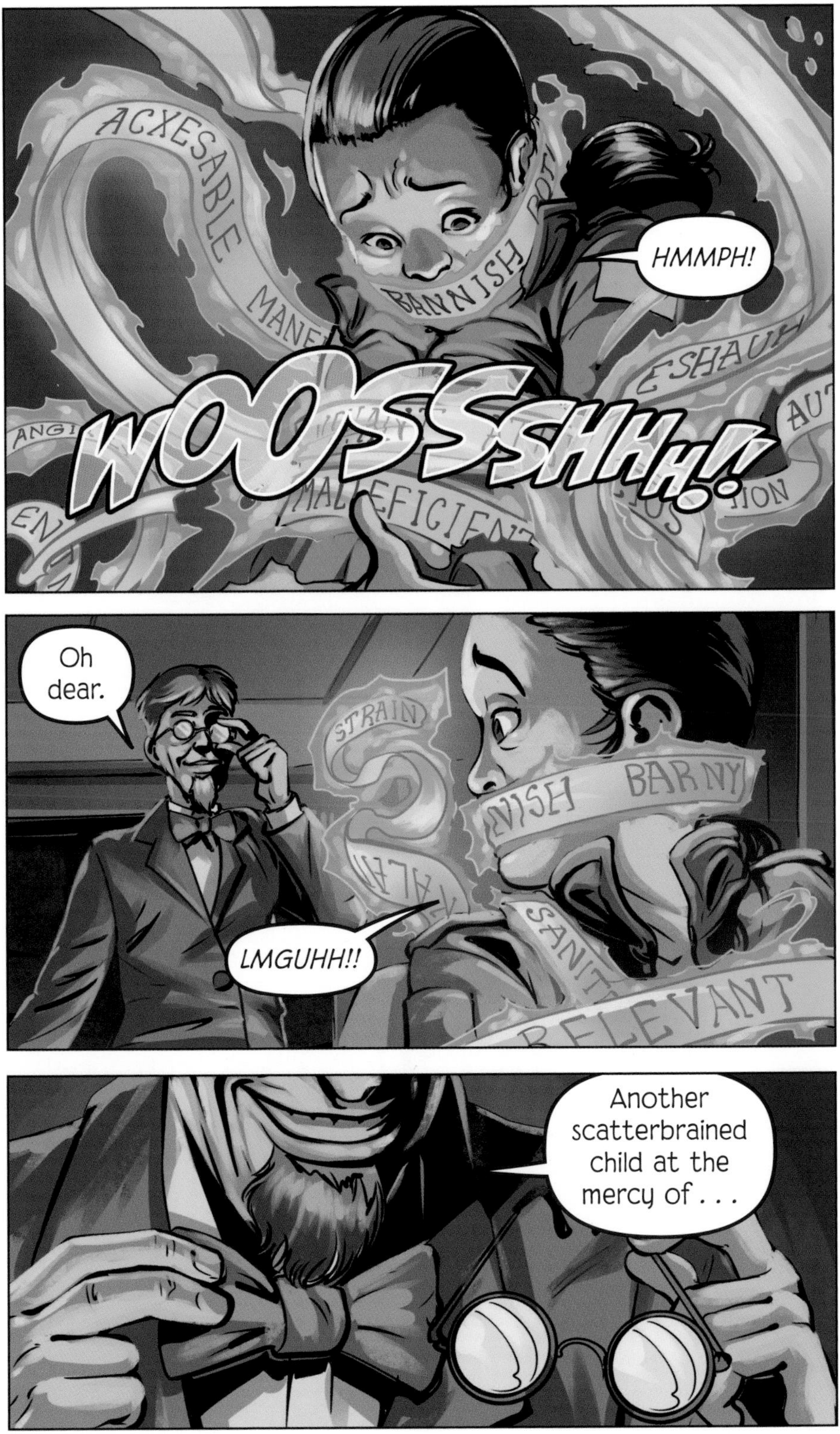
HMMPH!
WOOSSSHHH!!
Oh dear.
LMGUHH!!
Another scatterbrained child at the mercy of . . .

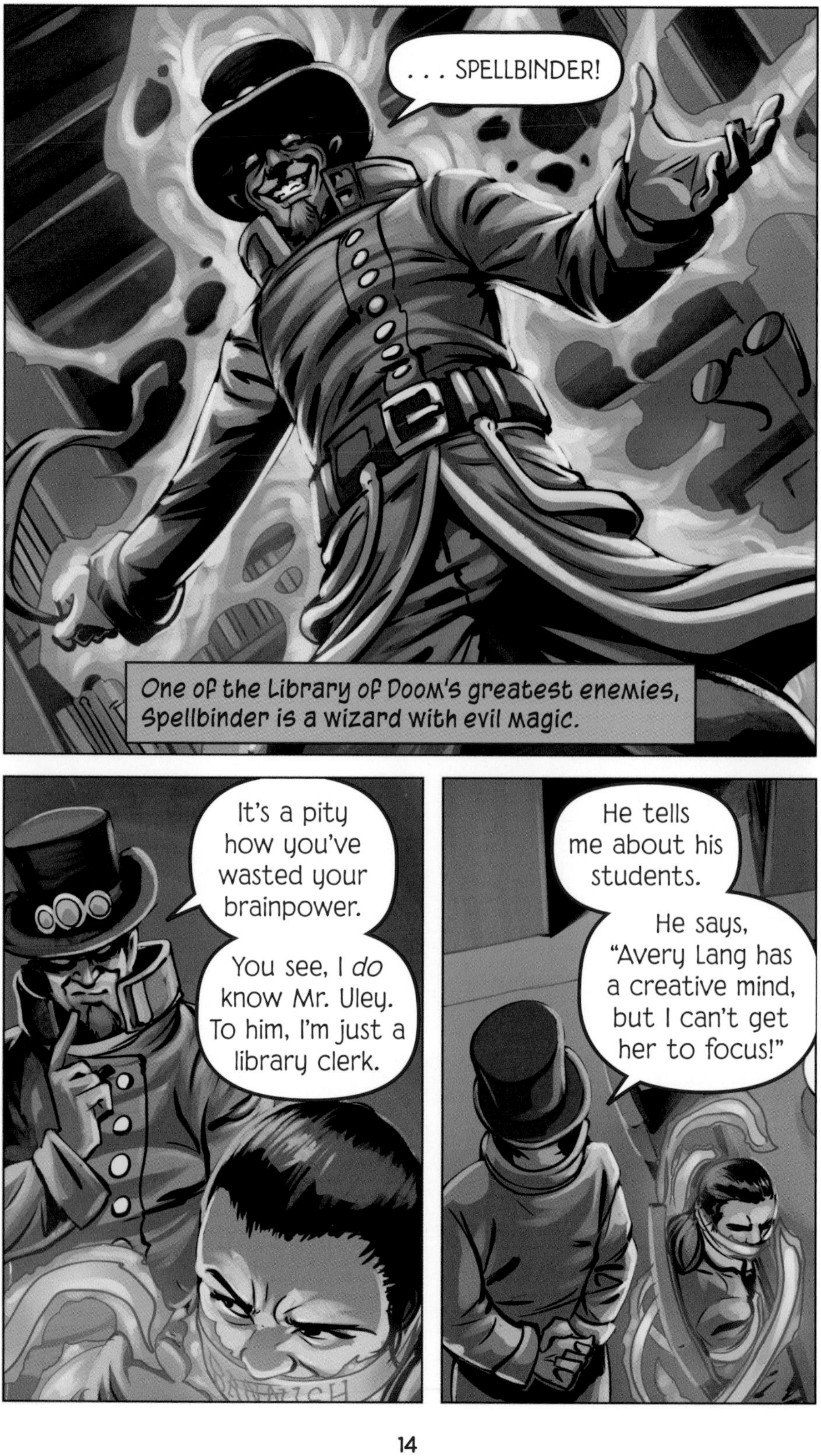
. . . SPELLBINDER!
One of the Library of Doom's greatest enemies, Spellbinder is a wizard with evil magic.
It's a pity how you've wasted your brainpower.
You see, I *do* know Mr. Uley. To him, I'm just a library clerk.
He tells me about his students.
He says, "Avery Lang has a creative mind, but I can't get her to focus!"

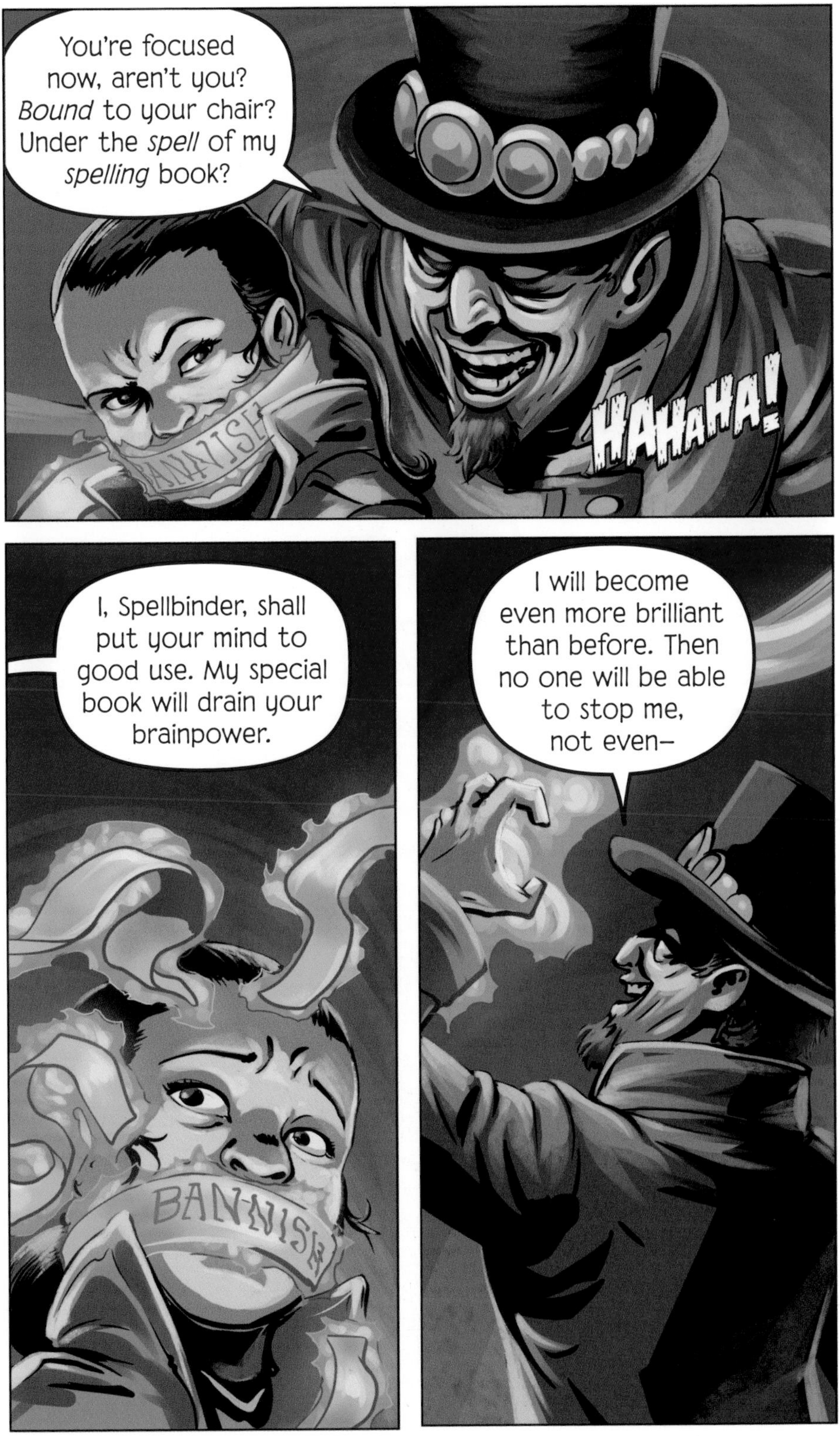
You're focused now, aren't you? *Bound* to your chair? Under the *spell* of my *spelling* book?
HAHAHA!
BANNISH
I, Spellbinder, shall put your mind to good use. My special book will drain your brainpower.
BANNISH
I will become even more brilliant than before. Then no one will be able to stop me, not even–

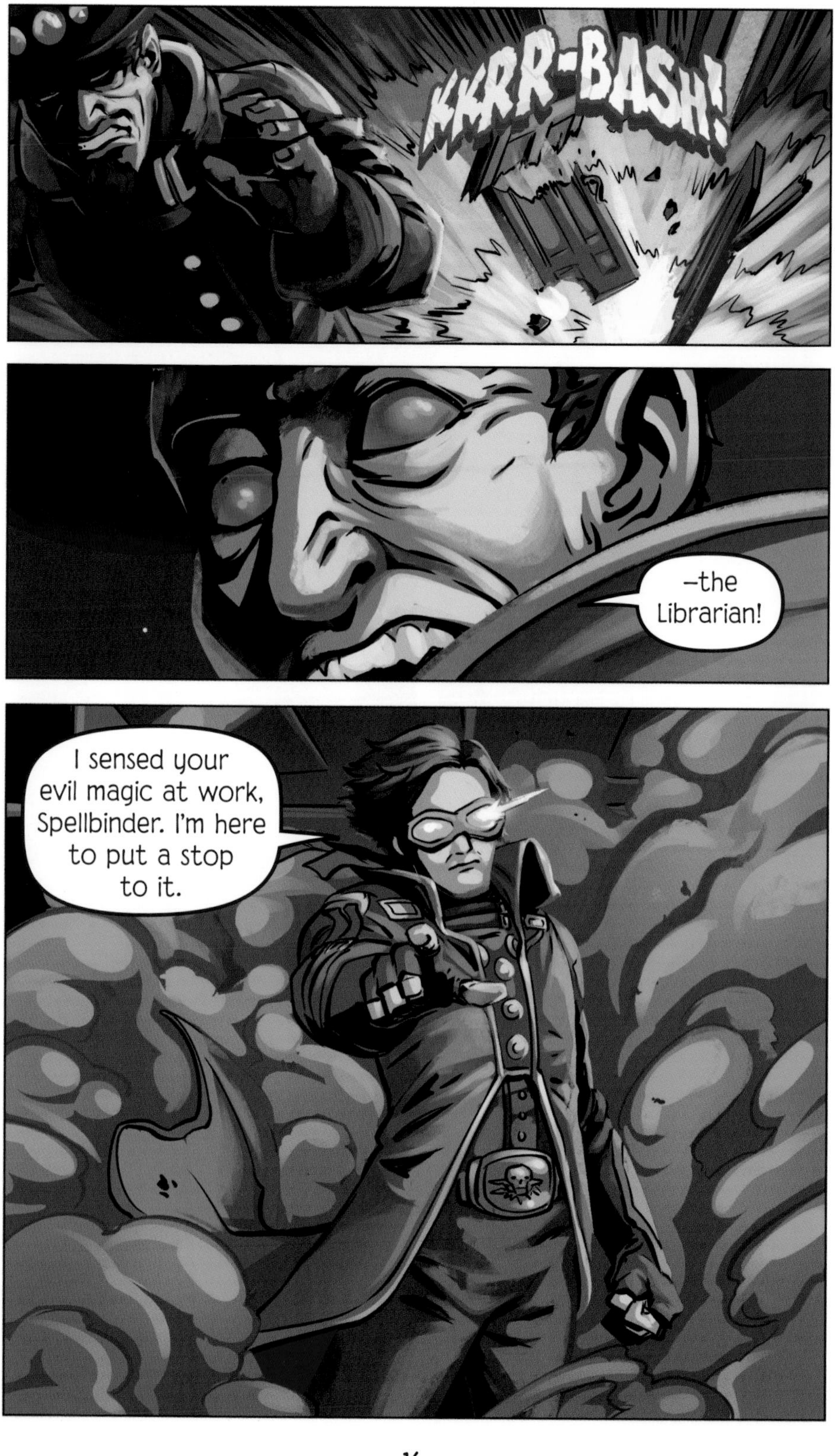
KKRR-BASH!
–the Librarian!
I sensed your evil magic at work, Spellbinder. I'm here to put a stop to it.

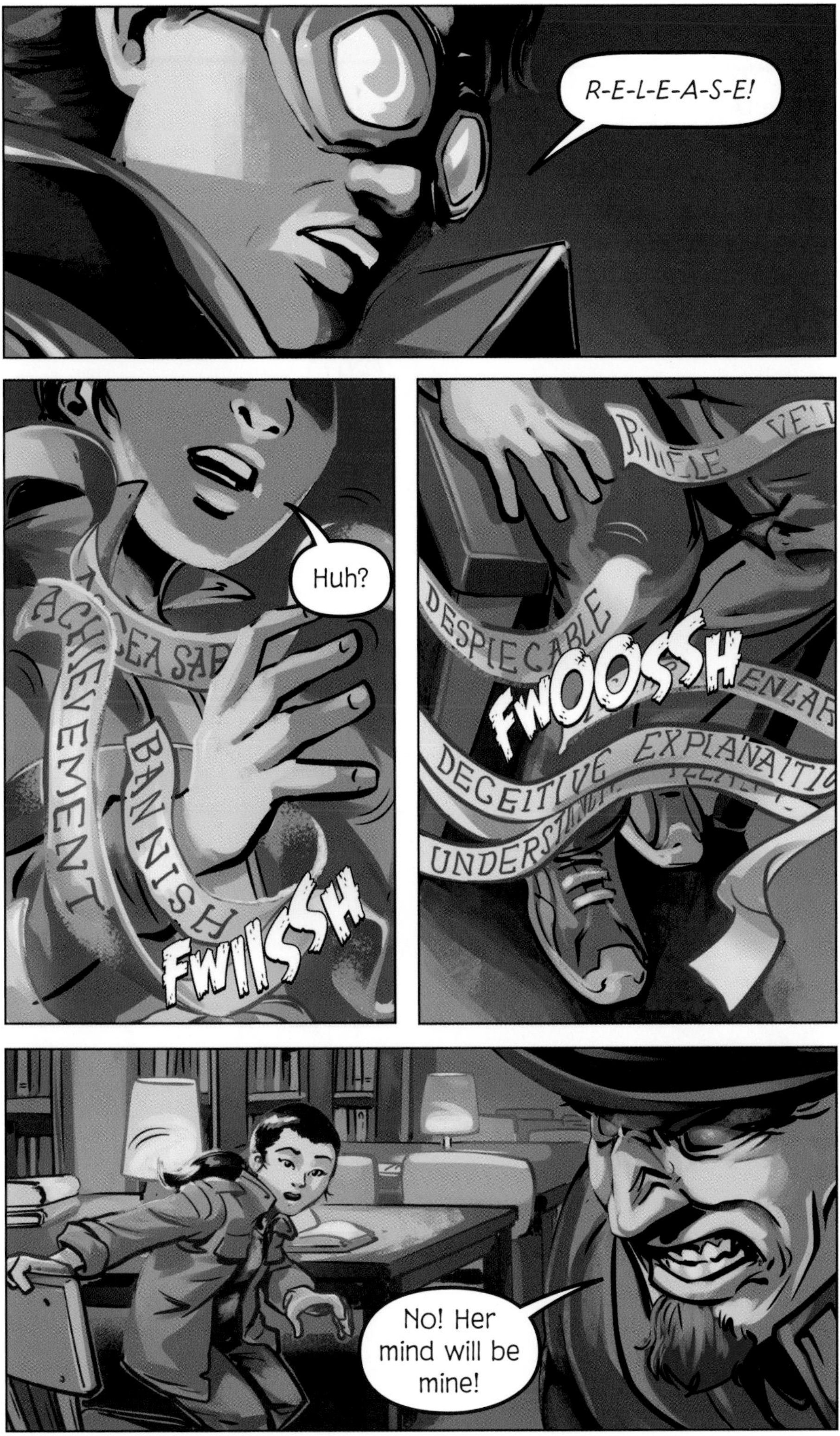
R-E-L-E-A-S-E!
Huh?
ACHIEVEMENT
BANNISH
FWIISSH
DESPIECABLE
FWOOSSH
DECEITIVE
No! Her mind will be mine!

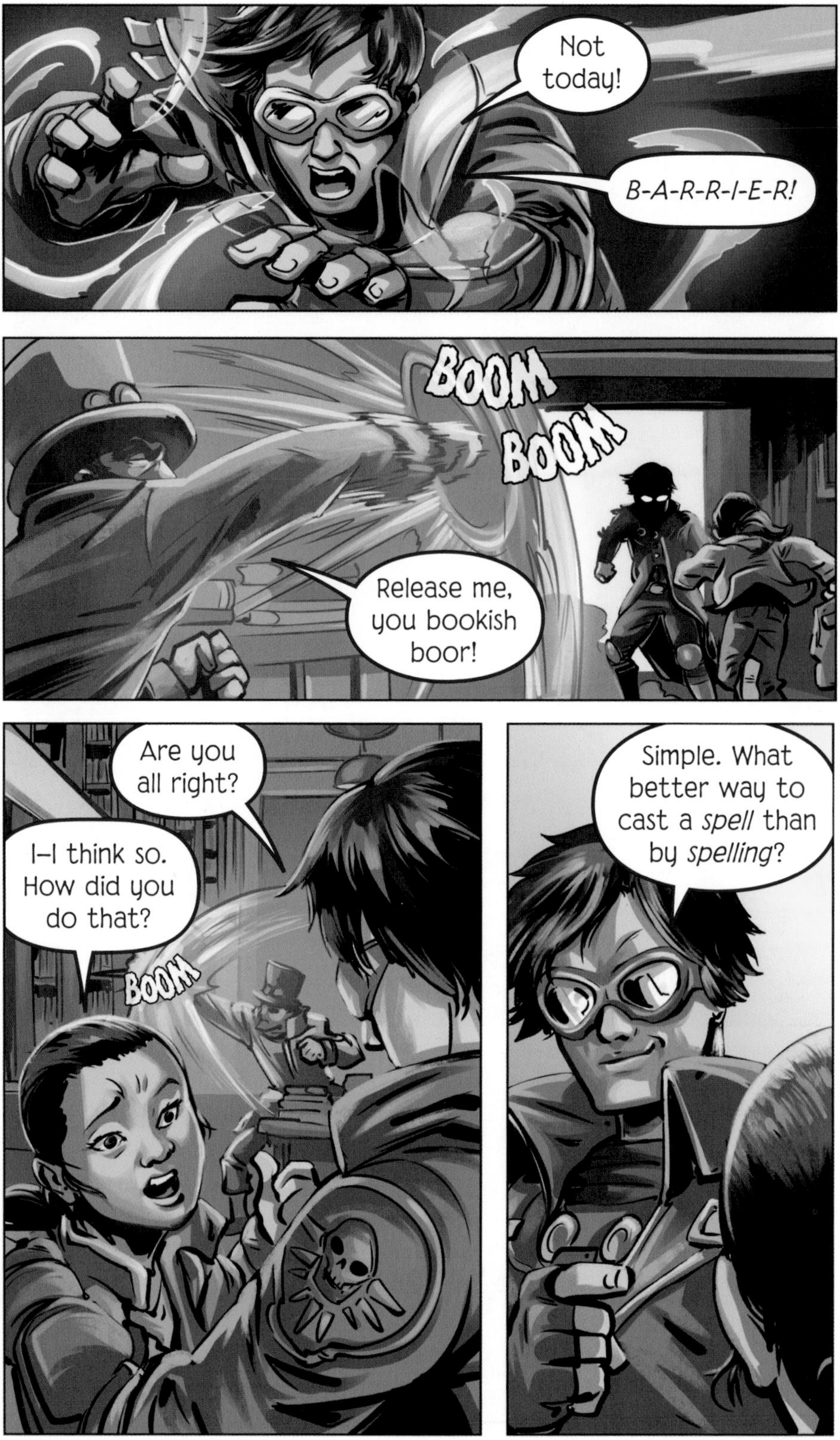
Not today!
B-A-R-R-I-E-R!
BOOM
BOOM
Release me, you bookish boor!
Are you all right?
I–I think so. How did you do that?
BOOM
Simple. What better way to cast a *spell* than by *spelling*?

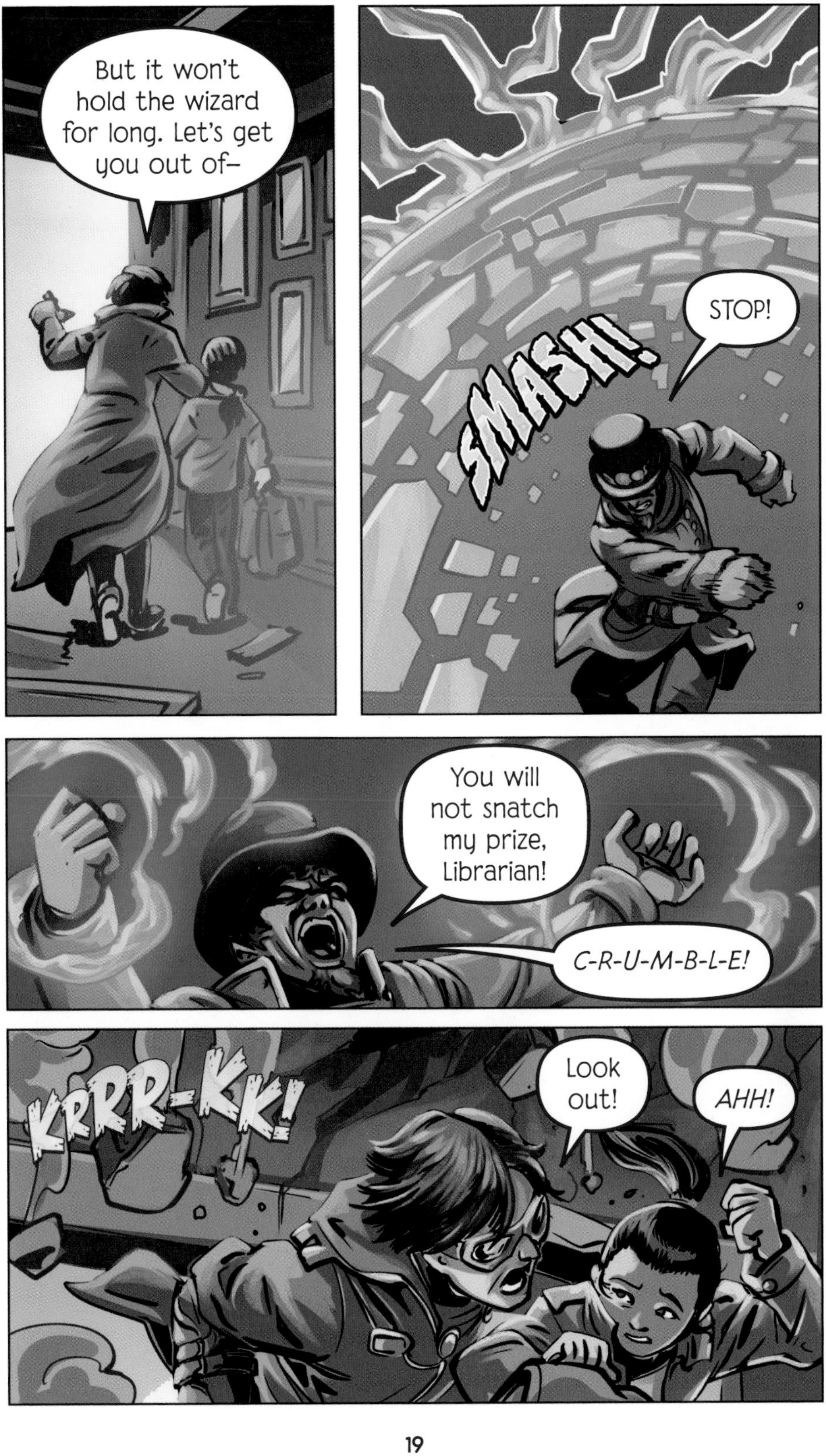
But it won't hold the wizard for long. Let's get you out of–
SMASH!
STOP!
You will not snatch my prize, Librarian!
C-R-U-M-B-L-E!
KRRR-KK!
Look out!
AHH!

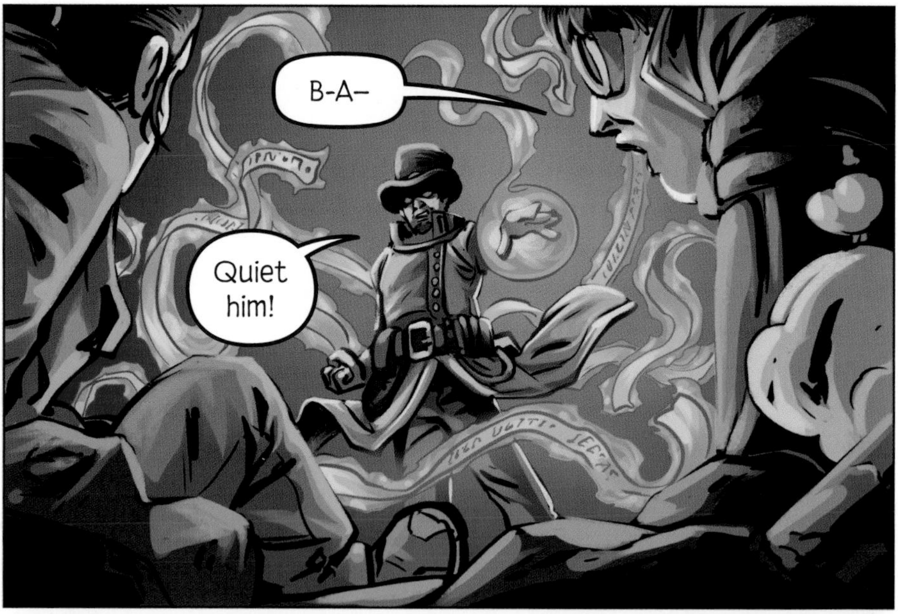
B-A–
Quiet him!

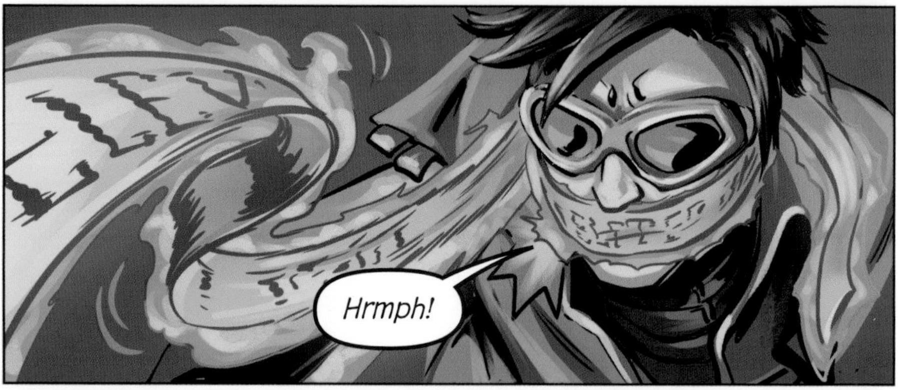
Hrmph!

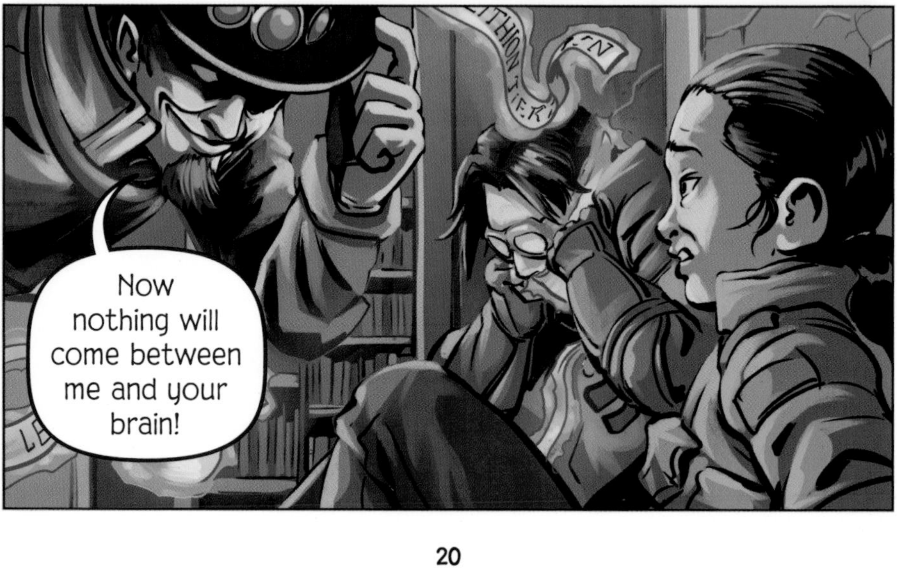
Now nothing will come between me and your brain!

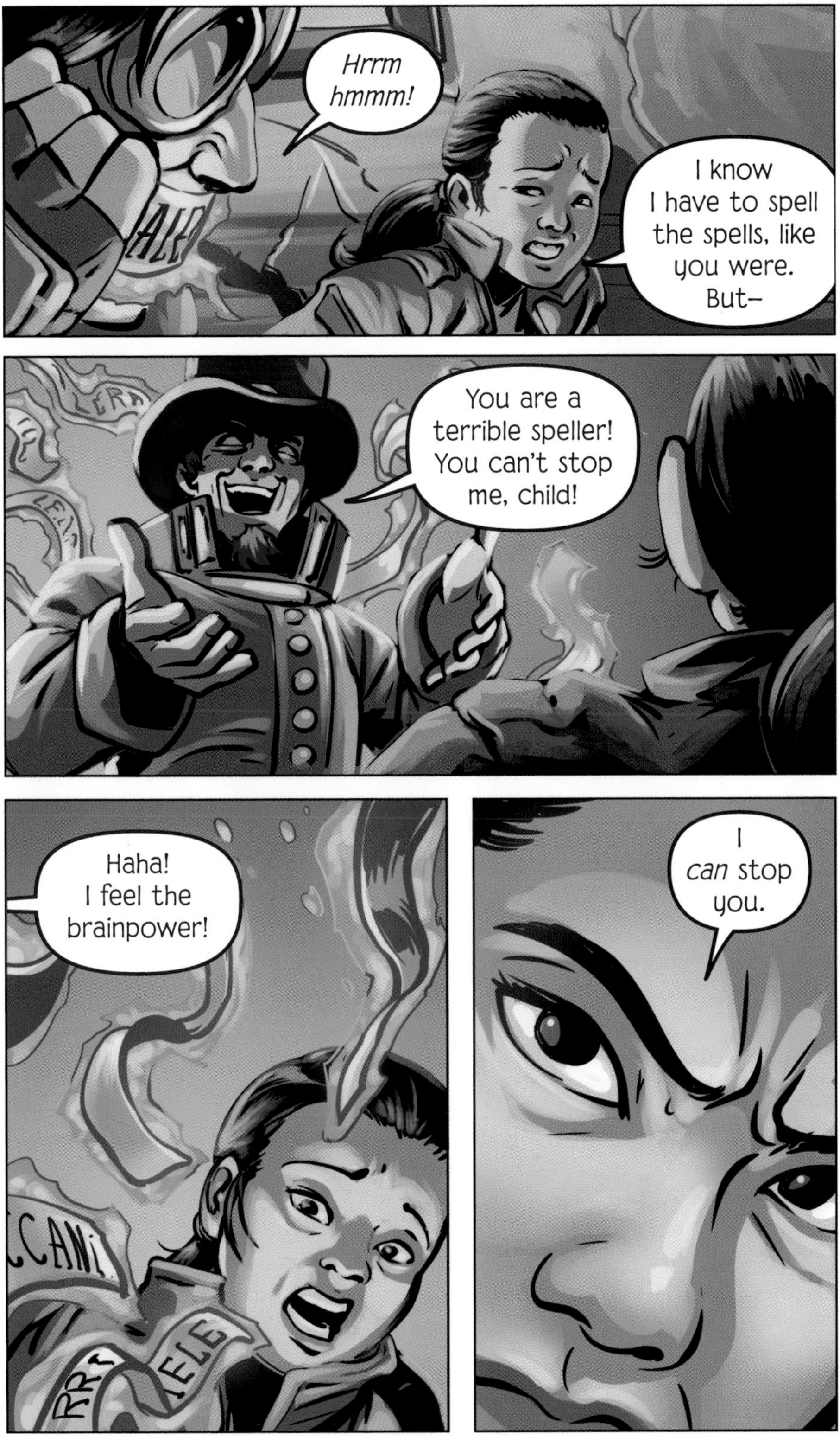
Hrrm hmmm!
I know I have to spell the spells, like you were. But–
You are a terrible speller! You can't stop me, child!
Haha! I feel the brainpower!
I *can* stop you.

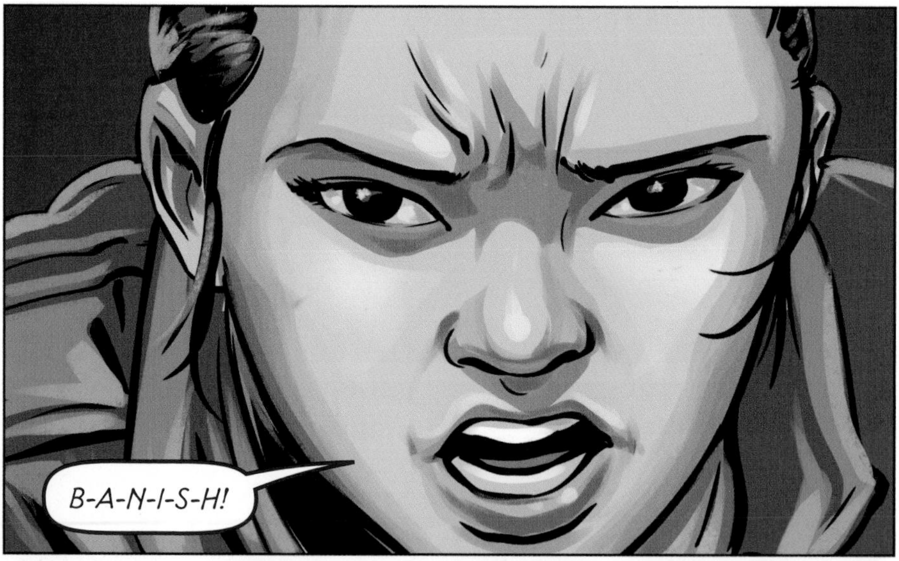
B-A-N-I-S-H!

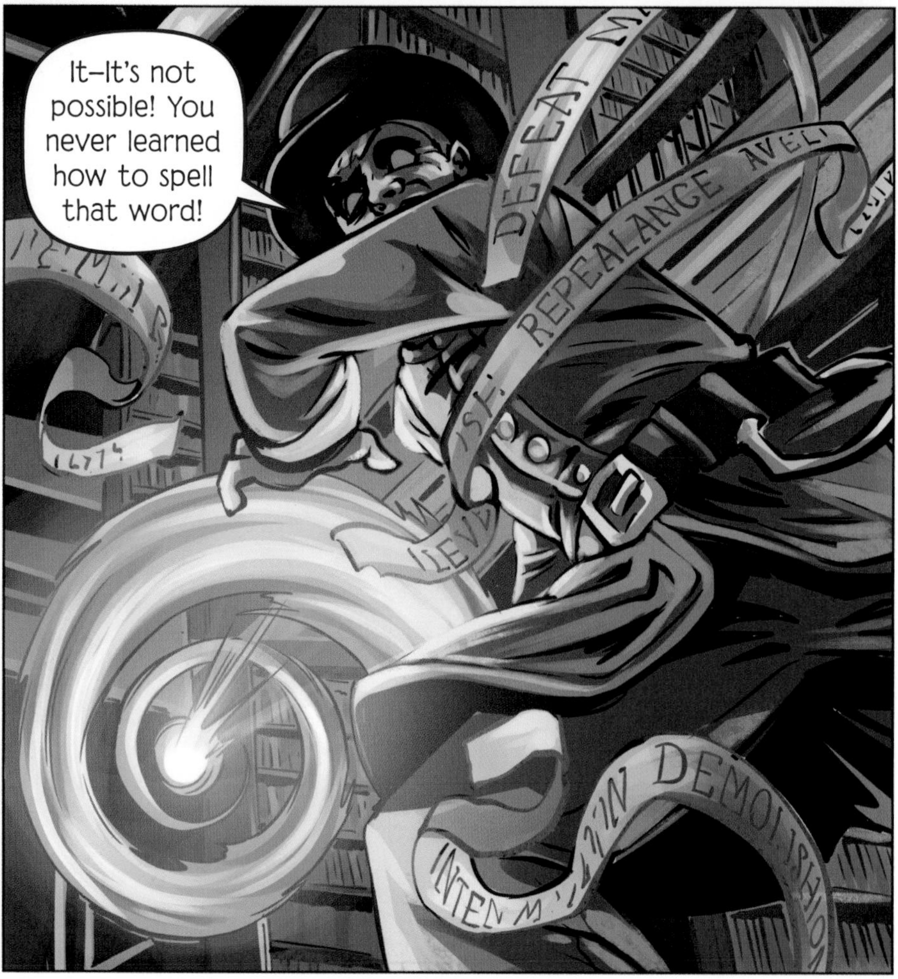
It–It's not possible! You never learned how to spell that word!
DEFEAT
REPEALANCE

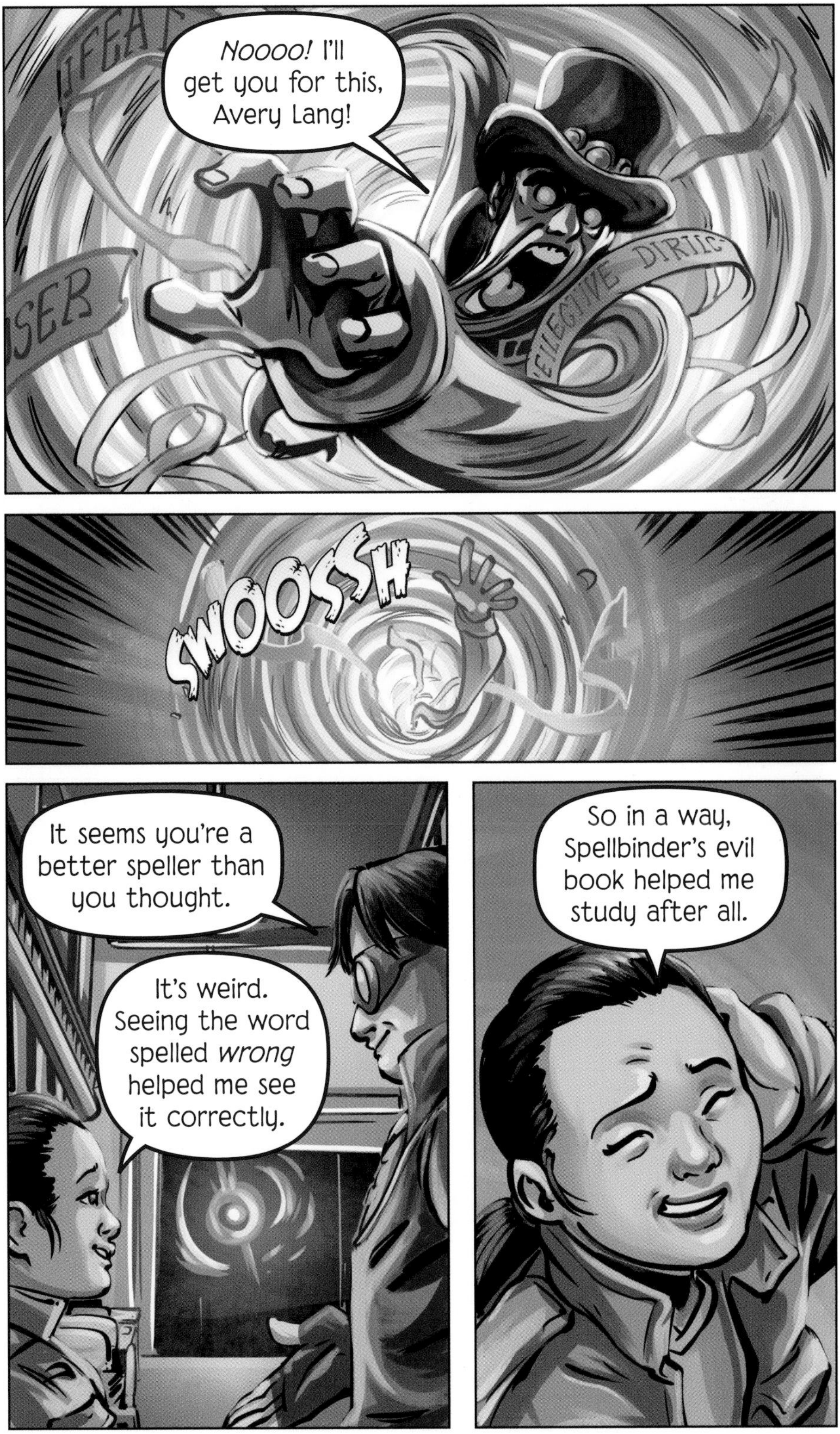
Noooo! I'll get you for this, Avery Lang!
SWOOSSH
It seems you're a better speller than you thought.
It's weird. Seeing the word spelled *wrong* helped me see it correctly.
So in a way, Spellbinder's evil book helped me study after all.

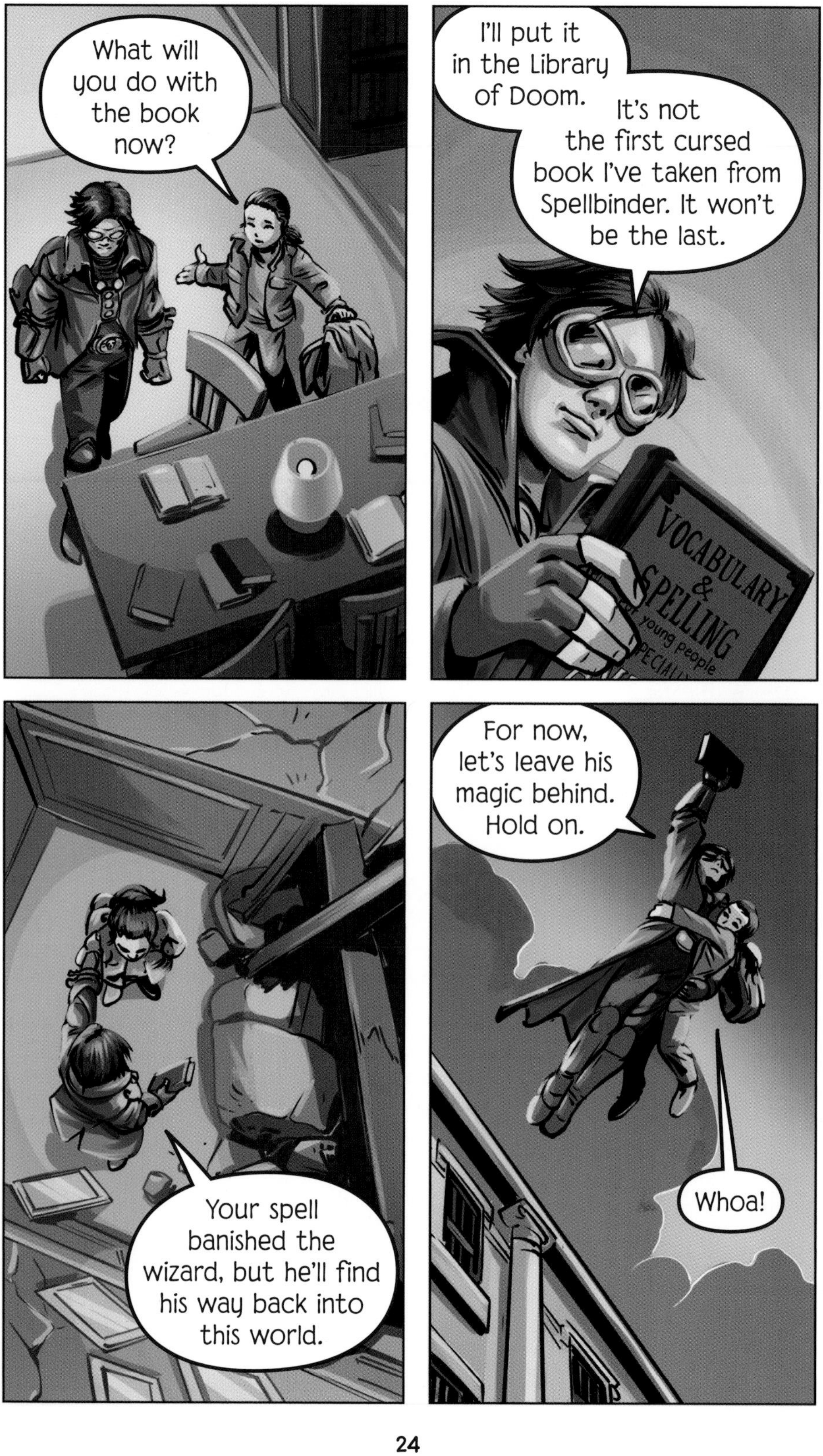
What will you do with the book now?
I'll put it in the Library of Doom.
It's not the first cursed book I've taken from Spellbinder. It won't be the last.
VOCABULARY & SPELLING
young people
Your spell banished the wizard, but he'll find his way back into this world.
For now, let's leave his magic behind. Hold on.
Whoa!

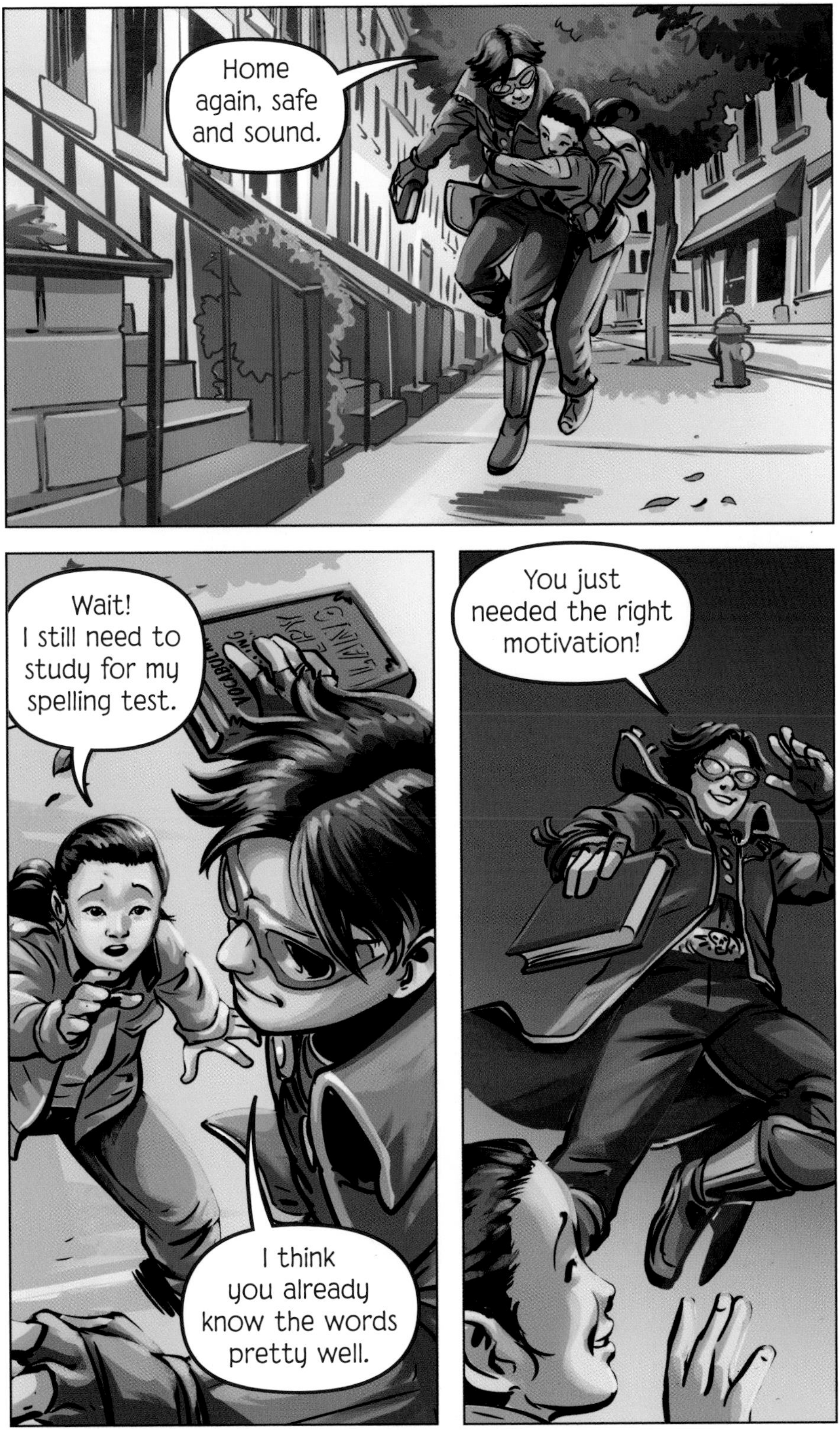
Home again, safe and sound.
Wait! I still need to study for my spelling test.
I think you already know the words pretty well.
You just needed the right motivation!

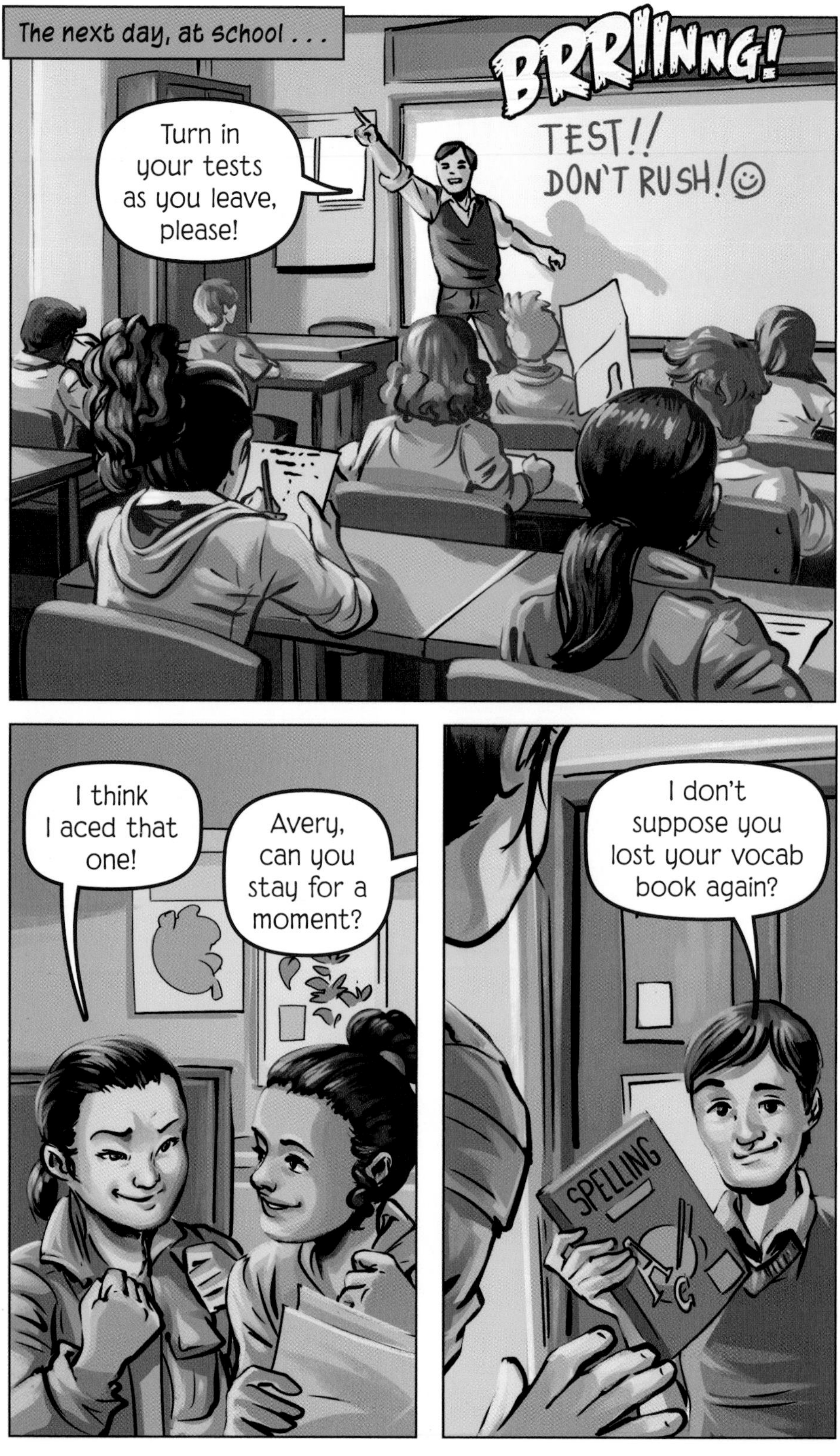
The next day, at school . . .
BRRIINNG!
Turn in your tests as you leave, please!
TEST!! DON'T RUSH!
I think I aced that one!
Avery, can you stay for a moment?
I don't suppose you lost your vocab book again?
SPELLING

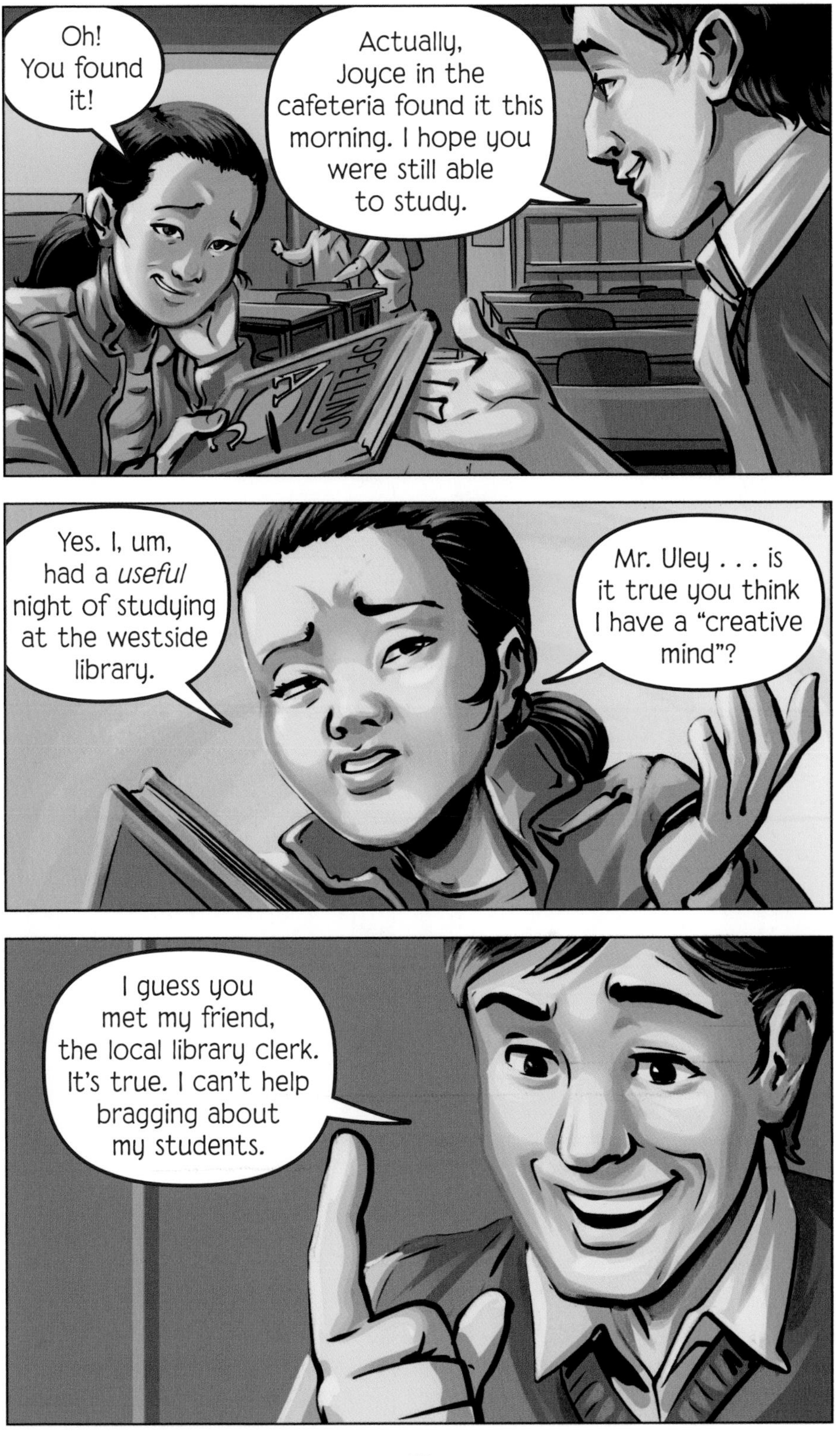
Oh! You found it!
Actually, Joyce in the cafeteria found it this morning. I hope you were still able to study.
Yes. I, um, had a *useful* night of studying at the westside library.
Mr. Uley . . . is it true you think I have a "creative mind"?
I guess you met my friend, the local library clerk. It's true. I can't help bragging about my students.

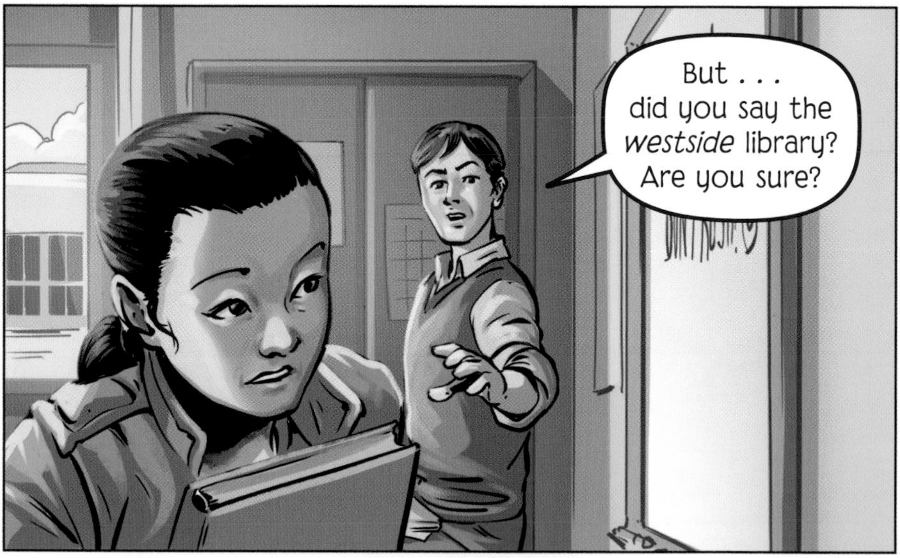
But . . . did you say the *westside* library? Are you sure?

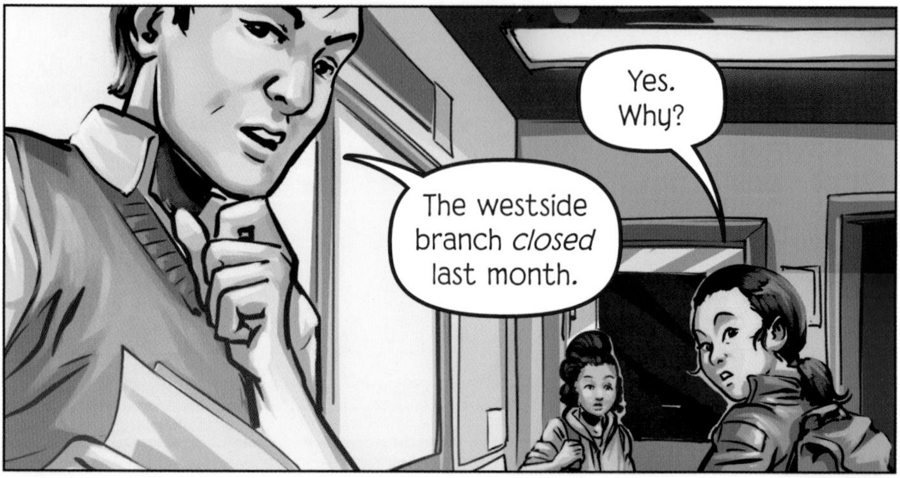
Yes. Why?
The westside branch *closed* last month.

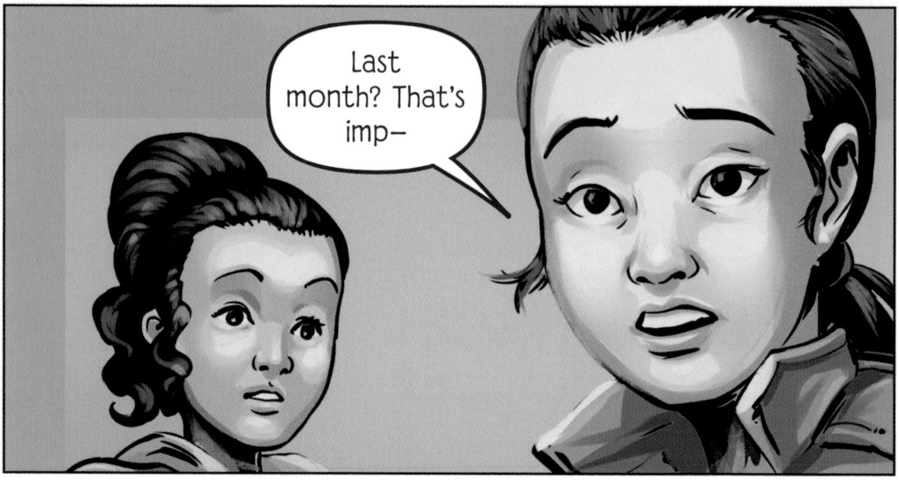
Last month? That's imp–

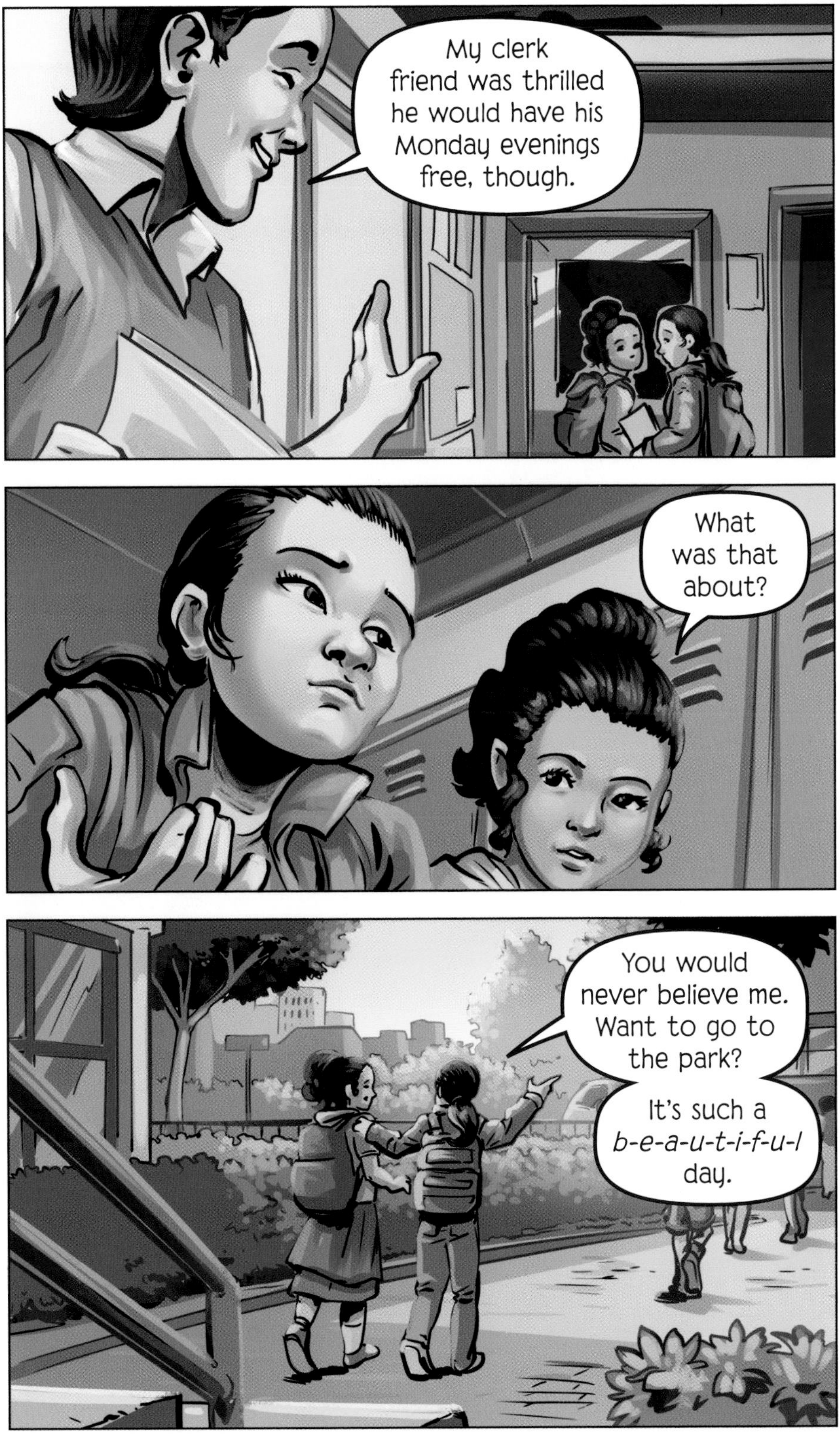
My clerk friend was thrilled he would have his Monday evenings free, though.
What was that about?
You would never believe me. Want to go to the park?
It's such a *b-e-a-u-t-i-f-u-l* day.

LOOK CLOSER

1

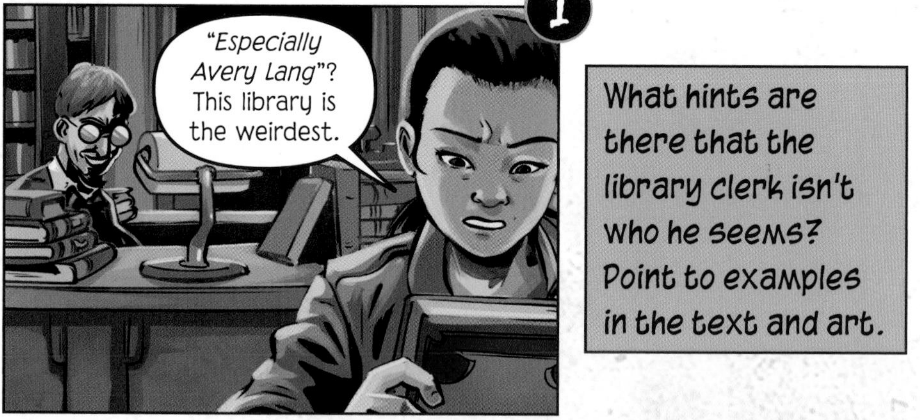
"Especially Avery Lang"? This library is the weirdest.

What hints are there that the library clerk isn't who he seems? Point to examples in the text and art.

2

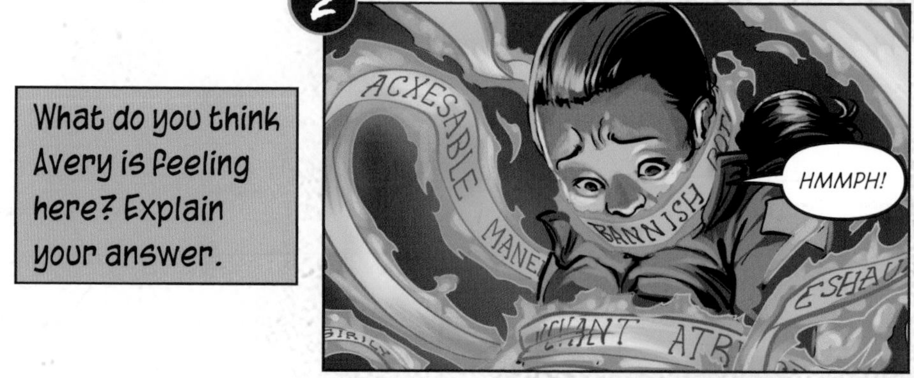
ACXESABLE
BANNISH
HMMPH!

What do you think Avery is feeling here? Explain your answer.

3

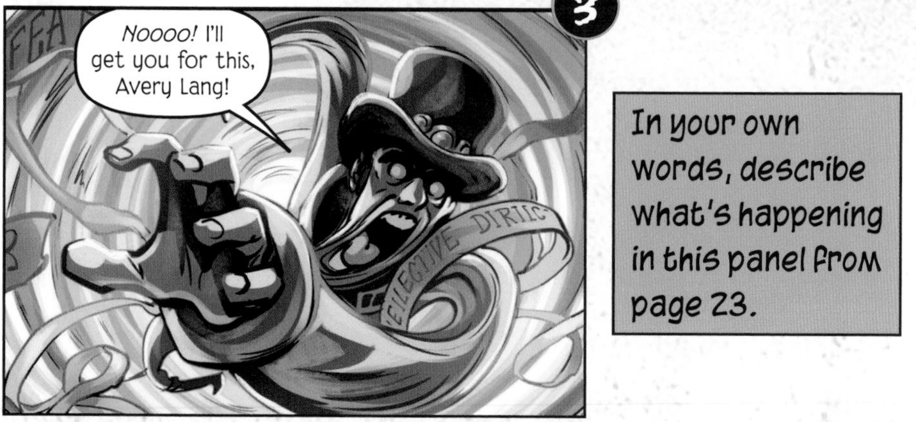
Noooo! I'll get you for this, Avery Lang!

In your own words, describe what's happening in this panel from page 23.

GLOSSARY

banish (BAN-ish)—to force someone to leave a place for a long time

barrier (BAR-ee-uhr)—something that stops movement from one place to another

boor (BOOR)—a rude person

branch (BRANCH)—a library, office, or other similar building in a neighborhood that is part of a larger organization

clerk (CLURK)—a person whose job is to keep track of records and do other general office tasks

cursed (KURSD)—under an evil spell that is meant to do harm

scatterbrained (SKAH-tur-breynd)—being forgetful and unfocused much of the time

spell (SPEL)—words that when spoken have magic powers; also, to say the letters that make up a word

vocabulary (voh-KAH-byoo-lar-ee)—the words that make up a language; also shortened to vocab

wizard (WIZ-erd)—a person with magic powers

ABOUT THE WRITER

STEVE BREZENOFF is the author of more than fifty middle-grade chapter books, including the series Field Trip Mysteries, Ravens Pass, and Return to Titanic. He has also written three young adult novels, *Guy in Real Life*; *Brooklyn, Burning*; and *The Absolute Value of -1*. In his spare time, he enjoys video games, cycling, and cooking. Steve lives in Minneapolis with his wife, Beth, and their son and daughter.

ABOUT THE ARTIST

JUAN CALLE is a former biologist turned science illustrator, trained at the Science Illustration program at California State University, Monterey Bay. Early on in his illustration career, he worked on field guides of plants and animals native to his country of origin, Colombia. Now he owns and works in his art studio, Liberum Donum, creating concept art, storyboards, and his passion: comic books.